THE CAMERA: BLOODTHIRST

By Eric A. Shelman

DOLPHIN MOON PUBLISHING

The Camera: Bloodthirst
is a work of fiction by
Eric A. Shelman

©2014 Dolphin Moon Publishing

ISBN 978-0-9891-4167-3

Print Version

Proofread by Megan O'Hara

Cover Art By Jeffrey Kosh

DEDICATION

There is no doubt that I first have to thank my brother, Don Shelman, for his help in the initial brainstorming for this novel. He lives in Harvest, Alabama with his wife Marion, and he is a super smart guy and an avid reader.

With regard to The Camera: Bloodthirst, I came up with the idea, but his enthusiasm often tells me whether it's a good idea or a shitty idea.

Thanks, Don, for not thinking *this one* was crap.

The thing is, once I present the idea and we talk through our initial analysis of the story and what the possible sequels to it could be, I don't like to give him much more. The reason? I want his first reading of the book to be fresh. Though he already knows the main premise of the book, I want him to really be able to experience the ride and see if it provides the intensity that I hope it will.

Now I must take a moment to thank my friend Dave Gammon, who, if you've read my Dead Hunger series and his reviews of all of my books on horrornews.net, you'll know he's a character in that book series, starting at book #2. He even gets his own, individual adventure in book #5.

We've actually even met two times, which is quite a change from most of my Facebook friends. I remember in the beginning pestering him to write a review of my book – not having ever spoken with him before – and he eventually did. From there, Linda and I have become close friends with him and his girl, Leona Skye.

Thanks, Dave.

That brings me to my wife, Linda. Nothing more needs to be said except that she supports the hell out of me and I love the hell out of her. Thanks, baby.

THANKS

There are always a few people I want to thank that aren't on my dedication page – hope you understand.

First off, there are some great fans out there who want to be involved in my beta reading group. Just to let you know, I've pretty much minimized betas and have gone the route of a proofreader. BUT because I love beta readers for storyline and to learn just how much they enjoyed the book, I'll never completely stop that process.

Allow me to thank Ramona Martine, who has been a VERY enthusiastic Facebook friend and reader. She pours herself into her reading and into her author promo. If you are an author and she is a fan, consider yourself lucky.

Giles Batchelor is a savvy dude, and he spots things that many others don't. He enjoys a good story and if he likes it, he's Ramona-ish in his promotion of it – or is *she* "Giles-ish?" Who knows? They both love reading and they are appreciated.

While *this* isn't a zombie story per se, it does have some elements of that world, so I'd like to say thank you to Jeff Clare, Danielle Pascale, Anna Dolhancryk, Rebecca Parker (whose story is featured at the end of this book!) and others from ATZ, or All Things Zombie on Facebook. They seem to take a personal interest in helping me forge ahead, and it is SO appreciated. Thanks to all of you. Special thanks to everyone at Zombie Book of the Month Club on Facebook, too. (Yep, I was the AUGUST 2014 winner!)

On the reader front, it's kind of intense how many fantastic Facebook friends are on my side. Laurie Mault, Jill Richards, Shannon Richards, Shannon Sharpe, Sara Anne Jones, Claire Rees, Lana Sibley, Tabatha Wheat, Debra Allen, Joseph Fleischman, Amanda Felix, Victoria Hansen, Leona Skye, Melissa Kendrick, Jim Cole, Helen Speirs, Julie and Scott Duncan, Dave Gammon, Chris Berget, Marion Shelman, Christopher Mahood, Vikki Solms, Denise Burns, Lisa Marie Williams, Erin Bailey, Barbara Friskey, Fran Mantuano, Kya Aliana, Tina Crum, Alina Lonescu, Julie Alton, Nichola Lines, Melanie Alexander, Tracey Poist, Lori Fontanez, Stephanie Lunsford, Tim Feely, Jeneice Townsend, Pheebz Pentenstine, Brett Shaw, Susan Hagy, Amanda Barnett, Monique Lewis Happy, Gary McCluskey, Erin Elizabeth, Chrystal Roe, Justin Dunne, Christine Cox, Brandy Havers, Aimee Kidd, Shellie Brewer, Valarie Smith, Richie Shiers, Nycole Kerrigan, Tami Kessler, Deborah Lee-Brown, Deanna Pitts, Baylie Poller, Dave Weirs, Linda McCampbell, Shannon Walters, Gavin Cooksley, Christian Erik Zavala-Ramos, Catrina Gustavsen, Dan Cercesa, Shannon Champion, Danielle Lowry, Eden Lowry, Bradley Thornton, Holly Zaldivar, Julie Greig, Sharon Berget, Erin Elizabeth, Carrie Herbel, Ruth Butterfield-Leatherman, Gerald Hughes Jr., Junie Baratti, Amy Flowers, Claire Riley, Traci Loya, Amanda Weeks, Dana Sachs Manley, Shelley Segree, Carolyn Carrie, Christine Cox, Sheree Ito, Louise Feagans, P Mark DeBryan, Kathy Pepper, Diane Sigler, KC Cochran, Veronica Smith, Sean Curry, Geri Callahan, Terri King, Rachel Aukes, Violet Baker, Belinda Thompson, Lorraine Versini, Edita Ramer, Tammy Beard, Colleen Wanglund, Candace Searles, Carmen Guthrie, Lydia Zavala-Ramos, Michael Clare, Lynn Hunter (Cuz!), Linda Tooch, Matt Laughlin, Amanda Gayle, Kara Boyce,

Lily Kersseboom, Samantha Harlow, Brian Menard, Linda Coffman, Tony Gilbert, Dan Williams, Jesse Donovan, Debby Zeman, Robin Rodwell, Angela Trewartha, Dave Trewartha, Nastasia Nazar, Pat Wike, Maricela Mascorro, Kyle Beardsley, Brian Lane, Mike Yowell, Diana Thomason, Megan White, Gail Briggs, Sydney O'Brien, Michele Heeder, Lori Hopkins, Justin Connors, Anthony Velez, Tara Harris, Jennifer Hosey, Britta Victoria, Jay Guthrie, Armin Busch, Tom Leeland, Michael Fisher, Janet Hannon, James Dean, Charmaine Pantelli, Elana Reed, Jess Reed, Rachel Reed, Lee'Anne Hardin, Mark Brady, Jacklynn Sizemore, Jeremy Hunt, Toni Lesatz, Mike Krantz, Aprille Shadowspeak, Deirdre Toby, Allyson Clayton, Julie Alton, Rebecca Babblings, Alina Lonescu, Rene Wood, Jen Batchelor, Mike Cushing, Sandy Almansa, Mysti Holsinger-Stitt, Wayne and Barbara Olsen, Anne Stephenson, Shaun Phelps, and last but definitely not least, CJ DeAndrea. If you were left off this list, I'm sorry. You are thanked, too.

On the fellow writer front, I'd like to thank Mark Tufo, John O'Brien, Shawn Chesser, Armand Rosamilia, Stephen A. North, Suzanne Robb, Candy O'Donnell, Catt Dahman, Ian Woodhead, Ian McClellan, Shana Festa, Jeffrey Kosh, Tony Baker, James Cook, Bobby Adair, Joe McKinney, Anthony Servante, Robert Chazz Chute, Heath Stallcup, Stephen G. Bynum, H.j. Harry, W.J. Lundy, Sue Julsen, Jason Welebny, Mike Evans, and ... while not technically a writer, she has assisted me with marketing ideas, so Tracy Tufo is included. The others have inspired and helped me.

If you looked for your name and did not find it here, allow me to take the blame and say ... THANK YOU.

THE CAMERA: BLOODTHIRST

Book One

PROLOGUE

Cape Coral, Florida – 1994:

Jaycee Park was located at the end of a street called Beach Parkway in a town that dies after 9:00 PM. It was now 11:30 PM and he heard her familiar footfalls before he spotted her. He had watched her many times before.

Gil Bellows was born on June 6, 1968. His mother had told him a number of times that on that same day, Robert Kennedy had been killed. She had always dreamed that the baby – little Gil Bellows – was the reincarnation of the caring politician. She believed it in her heart and gave him the middle name of Kennedy.

It never felt right. Gil began doing his own research. The kind heart of RFK did not mirror the darkness in his own; but the idea of reincarnation set him on the path to discover who he might have been.

Little did his mother know that a man named Dean Randolph Woods had died the same day; cut down by a seventeen-year-old girl who had escaped her bonds. She had been stripped naked, taken deep into the woods, tied to a tree and smeared with animal fat.

Somewhere in Pennsylvania, that had been. The fat that was supposed to have been a draw to the predator animals of the forest had allowed her to work the ropes loose before they got to her and she had followed a narrow trail in the moonlight to a cabin. When she saw his van outside the cabin, she knew she had not found salvation, but the deviant's home.

Janine Denton was naked and exhausted when she reached the cabin; she realized she had no choice but to kill him if she were to have any chance of escaping and reaching civilization again.

The clock on the kitchen counter ticked softly, and in the filtered moonlight Janine saw it was 2:12 AM. She moved with cat-like steps, her feet screaming from the many punctures and lacerations she had suffered through the brambled forest path leading to his cabin, her feet stained with the wild blackberries that grew there.

In the kitchen, she slid open a drawer and hit pay dirt. The knife drawer. She removed the largest one she could identify. Working her way through the hallways lit only by glorious moonlight, she pushed open the door to a bedroom, sure that he would appear behind her any second to end it all. If that happened, so be it.

But instead, she was met by his deep snores.

The first plunge of the knife sank deep into his neck, a warm spray of blood hitting her in the face and eyes, obscuring her vision. She did not stop then, for if the blood continued to pump the man was still alive.

Janine stabbed Dean Woods no fewer than sixty times before falling, exhausted, off the bed and onto the floor.

She lay there and sobbed for an indeterminate amount of time. Afterward, still nude and in a daze, she found his keys and drove the van to town. Once she saw traffic, she stopped the van and got out, collapsing in the middle of the street where she was found.

Police heard her story. She took them to the cabin and nearby, where she had been tied up, they found a tree festooned with body parts in various stages of consumption and decay.

Arms, hands, legs, heads, feet and torsos. All hung from the tree like Christmas ornaments, dangling from nylon rope. How he had gotten to some of the more far-reaching, narrower branches was not immediately clear to police, but the investigation would continue for a long time.

All of the dead victims had been female. Janine Denton wasn't one of them.

The last victim. The only survivor.

As for the girl running toward Gil at the moment, he didn't know her name; he had begun to call her Lorraine in his head, because if he were to name her after having just laid his eyes on her one time, that was what his mind would tell him. It was either that or Roxanne, the little blonde girl he fondly remembered kissing when he was just six years old. She had been his first.

No. Roxanne was too sharp sounding, though; not right for this girl. Lorraine had a sweet sound, like music. When he whispered the name in the night air, he could practically hear it floating on the breeze, drifting around to meet his ears again.

Gil closed his eyes. *Lorraine.* She needed no last name. He would know her intimately, but not for so long that it would matter.

As she approached, he zipped his jacket and pulled the hood over his head. It was the heart of summer and all the snowbirds had gone home. Most of the condominiums in the nearby mid-rise towers were vacant. He knew one that most surely was, for he had already used his swipe card to access the elevator. Before he left for the day, he'd slipped upstairs and used the master key he'd stolen from his supervisor to unlock the door of the penthouse suite.

The company for which he worked, Tyler's Specialty Painting, had won the bid to paint all of the units in the complex, as well as the common areas. Gil learned the penthouse was vacant for the long term when they began work there, working their way down to the lower floors.

They would be all alone on the deserted top floor – the eighth level. Right now, only two residents on the seventh floor lived there full time, and they were both as deaf as tree stumps. An old woman, probably in her eighties and widowed, lived a door to the right of the elevator. At the west end of the floor was an old man who always played Frank Sinatra at full volume. Fucker was probably closer to ninety years if he was a day.

As Lorraine approached, jogging close to the edge of the asphalt path, her reddish-blonde hair bounced in the faint moonlight. A distant boat purred along the Caloosahatchee River, but Gil focused on Lorraine.

She drew closer and he reached out, hooked his arm across her face, palmed the back of her head and

11

slammed her forehead into the trunk of the tree behind which he had been hiding moments before.

It had taken less than two seconds. The twenty-something-year-old had only had time to emit a brief squeal before her head met the bark of the old Spanish Oak.

Her eyes rolled back and her legs buckled. Gil caught her beneath the arms and dragged her quickly through the grass toward his old Toyota, zigzagging through all the plant identification signs telling visitors to the park what kinds of plants they were stomping on.

Okay, the car was his *mother's* Toyota. He lived with her in Lehigh Acres, but it was just temporary; a place to stay after getting out of a one-month stint in jail for a petty theft charge.

Gil knew he needed his own place. He had big plans, and none of them would happen in his goddamned mom's house. Edna Bellows was tolerant of him, but she would only take so much, and that did not include some of his favorite things.

Like this.

The two-door coupe was a rusty piece of shit and the lid of the trunk protested with some fervor when he opened it. He glanced briefly behind him and lowered her into the trunk, resting her inside the travel golf bag he'd picked up at the thrift store. It was nice and strong, but was made of lightweight canvas. Her small frame fit perfectly within. It was designed to hold a full, large bag filled with clubs, along with golf shoes, ball retrievers, and anything else a golfer might want to take on a plane.

Lorraine. He reached down and stroked her breasts through her tee-shirt, moist with her sweat from the jog. Gil turned and looked behind him again.

Nothing moved. He turned back, bent down and pressed his nose into her shirt, breathing in, filling his lungs. Standing upright, he closed his eyes and held the breath. It was *her* inside his lungs. It was Lorraine's very essence.

The brown, 1979 Celica may have been on its last leg, but it had enough juice to get his prize where he wanted her. He zipped the bag and closed the trunk, again eyeing the park before getting in the driver's seat, the driver's side door protesting as much as the trunk.

As he turned on the headlights and cranked the steering wheel hard to the left, movement caught his eye.

It was a man. He was holding something in his hands.

He was holding it up to his eyes. Gil put the car in gear and accelerated slowly, keeping one eye on the distant figure.

He listened for pounding from the trunk. There was none.

*****

Scanning the clouds overhead, Stan Richardson knew tonight would be a bust.

"Big surprise," he mumbled. Nothing was working out lately. Since the divorce, it had all been downhill.

He shook his head and eyed his bicycle as the light breeze picked up.

He looked again at the sky. "Great," he muttered.

The clouds had been a harbinger of the storm to come. The breeze turned into a wind and now the air in the park was alive with the sound of rustling leaves. White caps had already formed on the distant river, highlighted by streetlights from the Midpoint Bridge that spanned the mile-wide waterway.

He'd bought the 35mm Pentax K1000 as a birthday present to himself. He could only afford it because they were discontinuing the body and it was half off. Even then, by the time he'd bought the used lens he wanted, it was over a thousand bucks.

It was a full moon tonight, but with the cloud cover, it didn't seem bright enough to get any good night pictures. He had brought the filters the book said he should experiment with, and he'd loaded up high-speed black and white film, but with the moon obscured by clouds, his chances of getting any decent shots were slim.

Still, Stan didn't put the camera away. He raised it to his eye and scanned the park.

As he panned left to right, he stopped. Something was wrong with the shadows. He looked just to the right of what had caught his attention, and saw somebody standing there.

He lowered the camera, squinted to see, then raised it to his eye again. It was almost more crisp through the lens.

Stan turned and walked quickly to his bicycle, flipped open the satchel strapped to it and removed the zoom lens. He made the switch and this time he stayed on the sidewalk beside the bicycle, partially obscured by the moon shadow of a palm tree that soared forty feet above him.

It was definitely a man and he was standing behind a tree.

A faint sound. Footsteps. Instinctively, he stepped back, pressing himself more deeply into the shadows and saw a girl run out from Beach Parkway, cross 20th Place, and straight into Jaycee Park.

He raised the lens and twisted it until he saw the man clearly. He was big. Over 6'5" maybe. He'd been in the park a hundred times and could easily gauge the man's height to the tree. No doubt; he was beefy.

Stan Richardson was not a big man. He was, in fact, freakishly small, in his personal opinion. At 5'3", he was the butt of jokes in high school and college. Girls did not pursue him and he hadn't the confidence to go after them. His thick glasses didn't help either, and his premature baldness began at age eighteen, a cruel, final kick in the face.

He focused and snapped four photographs of the man's shape. It was better than nothing if he was up to no good.

The girl's running shoes hit the pathway as she jogged farther down the trail, closer to the concealed man.

Get over, get over! He thought, but she did not. He considered calling out, but should he? Maybe there was a chance he was misreading this.

He justified it this way. He was a frightened man; he always had been.

To his horror, as the girl drew alongside the tree, the man reached out, hooked his hand around the girl's neck and yanked her toward him, directing her face right into the solid tree. She collapsed in his arms as Stan felt a chill ripple down his spine. His heart pounded.

He was scared shitless.

The man dragged the girl out of sight for a few moments before he emerged again, beside a brown coupe Stan hadn't noticed before. He opened the trunk with his key and hefted the girl, lowering her inside.

What the man did next, Stan could not see clearly. He bent forward, then stood up straight, staring at the sky for a long moment. Next, he reached back inside the trunk and did something before closing it.

It was at that moment he turned and Stan felt exposed, even in the shadows. His paranoia intensified, but surely the stranger in the hooded sweat jacket could not see him from there.

Stan lowered the camera and let it hang from the neck strap. He did not move.

He dropped his eyes to the sidewalk and heard the car door close and the engine turn over.

Stay or go? Walk? Run?

Stan didn't know.

He stayed and pretended to be preoccupied. He would call the police the moment he got home. It was ten minutes to his house on the bicycle.

He *could* save her.

*****

Gil took slow, deep breaths as he pulled the car onto 20th and turned right. The bald man on the bicycle appeared to be merely acting as though he were distracted, busily digging into a pouch on his bicycle, not looking up as his car passed.

Gil turned on the lights then, guiding the car toward his originally intended destination, adjusting his rear-view mirror to catch what the man on the bicycle did behind him.

The man mounted the bike hurriedly and turned west on Beach Parkway. That was it. Gil had made his decision.

He had been seen.

Gil cranked the wheel to the right, threw it in reverse, backed up, and executed a three-point turn to make his pursuit.

He drove slowly as he turned the headlights completely off. When Gil reached the corner and turned onto Beach Parkway, the clouds broke for a moment. He saw the bicyclist pedaling like mad, already at the third street off Beach. Gil made the turn, quick to turn the headlights back on; this street connected to Del Prado, the main boulevard, and if the cops saw him cruising in blackout mode, they would check it out. Cape Coral police were bored. Especially after 9:00.

The rider had already turned the corner, so Gil accelerated to the street he'd gone down and pulled to a stop. He watched the bicycle rider.

The man made his first left. Gil removed his foot from the brake and turned, driving to the next corner.

From there, he watched the man turn into the driveway of a home in the middle of the block. He opened a screened entry door and walked the bicycle inside, allowing it to slam behind him.

17

Gil sat there thinking. Would he call the police? Did he actually see what had happened?

No problem. A loser out on a bicycle in the middle of the night didn't have a family most likely. Either way, he could not take the chance the man had gotten his license plate, and to make matters more urgent, Lorraine would be waking up soon.

I'll just change the venue. More privacy here anyway, probably.

Gil pulled the Celica onto the grass and down by the canal, where he parked. If someone came by, his vehicle would just be a shadow in the distance, perhaps owned by a fisherman come to do some catfishing in the local waterways.

Gil got out of the car and walked briskly to the stranger's home. A single light burned in the kitchen.

He had to hurry.

*****

Stan picked up the phone and lowered his hand to dial. Static.

Jesus, he thought. *The girl needs my help!*

Often after heavy rains, the lines got wet and such thick static clogged the transmission that calls wouldn't even connect. Right now he could barely hear the dial tone beneath the interference.

Stan pushed buttons on the phone. Even the tones were impossible to hear. He slammed the phone down. He had to hurry!

Realizing the camera pack was still over his shoulder he went to the side table at the end of the sofa and shrugged out of the strap. He put the bag on the table and opened it, removing the camera. It had been a bit misty out there, and he wanted to allow the camera time to dry rather than let the moisture seep into the high-end photographic equipment.

Stan hurried to the garage door and went inside, flipping on the light. The one car garage swam into view in the light of the 60-watt bulb, and he stepped down and turned to his right. Flipping the switch next to the side door, he unlocked it and stepped outside, into the radiance of the yellow bug-repellent bulb.

Bugs swirled all around it, flitting into Stan's face and he wondered what the hell the benefit of a bug light was when it still attracted bugs.

The single screw at the base of the plastic phone box was stripped, and he'd tried to close it with rubber bands. The damned phone man would come on occasion to fix it, but do you think he'd replace the box? Not on the last six trips he hadn't.

Job security, guessed Stan.

He flipped up the hinged lid and found the wires sopping wet as he had suspected. No wonder every time it rained he had to wait several hours before he could make a call. It was frustrating, yet he usually had the luxury of allowing them time to dry on their own. This time, a girl's life might be at stake.

He held up the plastic lid and leaned in to blow on the wires hard with his mouth. Feeling the spray of water on his hand, he blew again.

He did not notice the shadowed figure pass behind him and into the garage.

ERIC A. SHELMAN

*****

Gil had already clipped the crucial telephone wires leading from the box to the overhead lines. The man could play around drying the inside of the box all he wanted; it would offer no solution now.

While the short, bald man blew into the box, Gil slipped silently behind him on soft, moist dirt, into the garage. The house next door had lights on and he could hear the sound of the low television within; if he were to kill him now, things could go even more wrong than they already had.

Gil stepped inside the garage and moved quietly behind the grey, Ford Taurus.

Moments later the man came back in. Gil eased himself up, watching the man's progression through the Taurus' windows as he moved through the garage. He had already sized the short man up. He would be child's play to take down.

Gil's only concern was that the captive in the trunk of his car was still unconscious.

*****

As Stan entered the garage, his eyes fell to the floor and he stopped dead in his tracks. Ahead of him, on the concrete, were muddy footprints.

Not his own. He had not gone back in yet, and had also wiped his feet on the mat just inside the door.

A chill shot down his spine. He rubbed his bald head and resumed walking, doing everything in his power to appear natural. His eyes moved to the footprints that disappeared around the corner of the Taurus' right front fender.

Stan turned his eyes to the laundry room door and went inside the house, closing the door softly behind him and turning the thumb lock.

*****

When the man stopped, staring at the floor of the garage, Gil could feel the man's panic as he gaped at what must have been Gil's footprints.

The distinct sound of a door locking broke the silence of the garage. Gil realized he needed to get to him now, and since the homeowner probably knew someone was hiding in the garage, he would exit the front door to go for help.

Gil ran-walked around the Taurus again and unlocked and opened the side garage door. He maneuvered through the side and made his way in front of the garage. He rounded the corner just in time to see the front door cracking open.

Gil charged for the screened entry, pulling the aluminum-framed screen with one fast motion and hooking his fingers around the entry door that was swinging toward him.

The minute he yanked the door open, Gil had a split-second to see surprise register in the man's eyes before he slammed his fist into the bald man's face, sending him staggering backward. After two stutter-step stumbles, he fell.

The small man's head hit the floor with a hard thud and his body slid another three feet before coming to rest, motionless. Gil grabbed the lamp on the hall table, jerking the cord from the wall and raising it high over his head. He brought it down into the man's face and the porcelain shattered, opening multiple gashes there that leaked blood onto the floor.

The crash sounded loud to Gil, but everything seemed amplified now; the mere situation likely intensifying his auditory senses.

He glanced behind him, breathing hard. No neighbors walked their little terriers along the sidewalk; nobody in sight. He closed the door softly behind him. He stared down at the bleeding man, who was either unconscious or was pretending to be.

Gil approached him and knelt down. His chest rose and fell steadily. The slow-spreading pool of blood that had formed just beneath his head grew larger, and small blood bubbles were blowing from his lips.

The bald man had been struck hard and he was really out. The lamp had taken care of the rest. Gil lifted an eyelid. The pupil rolled back.

Yes. He was out like a light, and he would be, possibly longer than Lorraine.

He made a choice, leaving the man for now.

His princess was waiting.

*****

Before he went outside, Gil searched the house briefly to make sure nobody else was home; a roommate or a wife or girlfriend.

There was a fireplace with some feminine looking stuff on the mantle. Maybe just family heirlooms; it didn't mean much. He disregarded it.

In the closet he found only men's clothing. All looked to be for the size of the guy lying on the entry floor.

Gil moved back toward the door, eyeing the camera on the table as he passed. Was that what the guy had been carrying? He made a mental note to remove the film in case the snoop had taken any photos of him.

He returned to his car parked in the vacant lot. He got inside, started the engine and pulled it up to the house, backing it into the driveway. Gil angled the trunk toward the entry walkway. No front plates were required in Florida, so no license plate would be visible from the street that way.

Sure enough, the bag was stirring when he opened the trunk, and when the girl inside sensed his presence, she screamed. Gil quickly leaned forward, grabbed her head and pulled it up, slamming it back into the floor of the trunk.

She fell still again. He leaned in and scooped the entire golf bag into his arms, lifting her out of the trunk. Closing the hatch, he stepped briskly up the walk.

In another fifteen long seconds carrying the unwieldy bundle, he stepped into the house. The entry was bare except for a pool of blood the size of a dinner plate, with several drops of blood leading off to his right.

The bald man was gone.

Excruciating pain that seemed to come out of nowhere made his head feel as though it had exploded, and suddenly Gil Bellows could see nothing but red-black spots dancing, followed by darkness.

*****

A sound. The screen door slamming?

Stan's world spun around him as he saw and felt the blood on his face. The taste of metallic copper assaulted his tongue.

The girl!

Adrenaline charged through his system as Stan struggled to his feet and sought a weapon. His feet slipped in his own blood as he wiped more of it from his eyes and staggered toward the fireplace.

The poker. He grabbed it, fumbling to clean his slippery hands on his soaked shirt.

He staggered toward the front door, the poker raised, and heard the outer screen door close again. Rivulets of blood ran down his face, dripping onto the floor, and he vaguely realized the entire front of his shirt was soaked with it.

Stan blinked. When he opened his eyes, the man was right in front of him, coming through the door holding a body-sized bundle on his shoulder.

Stan held his breath as the intruder, confusion plastered on his face, stared down at the bloody tile floor where Stan had lay unconscious just seconds before.

He turned toward Stan and with the last bit of strength administered through blurred vision, he rammed the poker forward, able to see it pierce the attacker's eye and keep moving.

24

Stan twisted it and tried to withdraw the fireplace tool, but he was weak, his hands too slick with blood. Still he pulled, feeling his fingers slipping from the brass handle. The log hook had clearly gotten lodged within the man's skull.

Dizziness overcame Stan and he released the poker and tripped backward over the coffee table, landing on the sofa. As Stan stared through the floating black spots that obscured his vision, the intruder carrying the bundle fell backward, the shaft of the poker protruding from his eye knocking into his precious Pentax. The camera toppled from the low end table and landed beside his would-be killer's twitching arms and legs.

Stan's world went black.

*****

"Help! Help!" shouted Belinda Callahan, from within her canvas prison.

Moisture had begun to seep through the material, and she could tell she was no longer in the trunk of a car, where she had determined she was earlier, before being knocked unconscious again.

The back of her head hurt, but not too bad. She reached behind her head and felt there, but no sticky muck found her fingertips. Whatever the moisture was, it was not coming from her.

She blinked her eyes repeatedly before noticing a small pinprick of light. She worked her finger up to it and pressed outward. She felt a zipper with her finger.

The hole got bigger. The zipper was lowering!

She got her whole finger through and pushed it slowly down, careful only to move the single digit and her arm as she opened the slot wider and wider.

A man's feet came into view and she braved the opportunity to pull the opening wider.

No movement at all. Belinda slowly unzipped the bag in which she had been confined lower still, until she could manage to sit up.

She gasped and screamed involuntarily. Tears came. If the person who did this was here, she might be living her last few moments.

What appeared to be a fireplace poker protruded from the eye socket of the man lying on his back. The other eye stared, sightless, toward the ceiling.

She turned away and screamed again. On the sofa was a man, slumped to the side. Where his head had been was a large, dark stain, running down the back cushion. His eyes were also open. He was clearly dead.

Belinda forced herself to her feet, tore open the door and ran into the street, screaming at the top of her lungs for help.

Help came. She collapsed into shuddering sobs at its arrival.

*****

The Pentax lay in the blood of Gil Bellows, a rapist and killer of six young women and a single man – Stanley Allen Richardson. As the warm blood flowed around the lens and into the cracks of the camera, finding its own path, it seeped into the body where eventually, it clotted and dried to a dark brown.

26

Although the crime scene was processed thoroughly, the bloody Pentax was never found.

When the inexperienced rookie cop burst in the door, his hands shaking with the gun held aloft, his boot kicked the edge of the 35mm camera. His adrenaline was such that the contact with the camera went unnoticed, and it slid cleanly beneath the end of the sofa.

Later, after the crime scene had been released and the family had been notified, an estate sale was arranged by the family. They only wanted to move on, and most of them felt that Stan was truly in a better place.

*****

Irvin Wilford was thirty-two years old. He had a fine wife named Jean, and four kids. Three boys and a girl. Two boys had come first, then a girl. The last boy, Eric, was to have been a girl, but then again you can't plan stuff like that. Nature runs its course.

Irv was 6'5" tall, which gave him the advantage, not only in the legal world – he was a criminal attorney – but also in everything he did. Every venture in which he became interested was possible for a big man, especially one with brains.

But folks didn't find out about his smarts until later, and that was okay. People were just more likely to show him respect and listen to what he had to say because of his height.

Irv wasn't extraordinary looking; he had dark, curly hair and he was far too thin. He had a substantial gap between his two front teeth, but they were straight, thanks to the braces he wore as a boy. He had intense, blue eyes and a smile and sense of humor that normally sealed the deal before anyone actually knew there was a deal.

His kids, Don, Gary, Janice and Eric, were 12, 11, 9 and 7, respectively. He never saw them. Not with the conferences and golfing and all the rest of the schmoozing he had to do on a regular basis.

Irv had heard about the murder down off Beach Parkway, so when he saw ESTATE SALE signs planted on Del Prado Boulevard, with arrows pointing down Beach Parkway, he put two and two together. It had been three weeks since the murders, which made sense. The family wanted to sell everything and put it behind them.

Irv's curiosity got the better of him and he slid into the left-turn lane of Beach Parkway.

It was just before noon on a Friday. Saturday would be the big sale day, so Irv was glad he'd seen the sign.

He pulled up in front of the home and parked. Another car pulled up behind him, so he put the Chevy Malibu in park and got out, sure to beat the other bargain hunter with his long stride.

He owned a small document camera that he loved to use for everything but documents. He told his kids it was a spy camera, which they thought was pretty cool, and he had used it to shoot documents on occasion; usually the docs he wasn't supposed to photograph.

A man and a woman walked through the house answering questions for the four or so people trotting through the house. Irv looked for bloodstains, but didn't find any. Floor was tile, so he eyed the grout, to no avail.

He spied a camera on the dining table, placed there beside stacks of dishes and some table lamps, all with dangling, white price tags.

He approached what appeared to be a 35mm camera, sitting atop its rigid, leather case, the zoom lens attached.

He went straight for it, picking it up.

"That one seems pretty new," said the woman, walking toward him. "From what I understand it's a good camera."

Irv glanced at her, then smiled and held out his hand. "Irvin Wilford," he said. "Folks call me Irv. And you are?"

The woman beamed, looking up at him. She was in her late forties or early fifties and was dressed as though about to attend a funeral. Perhaps out of respect for the dead man who once lived in the home.

"I'm Sandra Richardson," she said. "Stan was my brother."

"Well, I'm so sorry to hear what happened," Irv said. "I hope he didn't suffer."

She shook her head. "Are you interested in that?" she asked, nodding toward the camera in his hand.

"I already have several cameras," he said, holding the viewfinder up to his eye. "Hmm," he said. "Looks like the lens is out of whack. That's going to cost a pretty penny to set right."

"Really?" she asked. "Oh, that's a shame."

"It is," he said, putting it down and pretending not to be interested in it. There was nothing wrong with the camera at all that he could see.

29

"Excuse me, Irv," said Sandra. "What would you give for that?"

"Most I could justify would be ... how about $25.00? It'll cost me a couple hundred just to get it working properly," he said.

Sandra smiled. "Sold sir, and I truly appreciate it. That is one more item we can put behind us as we all try to forget this horror."

Irv moved toward her and put his large hand on her shoulder, squeezing it gently. "Sandra, this too shall pass. Time heals all wounds."

Irv could not think of any more wise sayings, so he opened his wallet, peeled a twenty and a five from within, and put the bills in the woman's upturned palm.

"Thank you, Irv," she beamed.

"Thank you, Sandra. But you look like you might just prefer to be called Sandy."

"I do when I'm at the beach," she said, smiling again, a blush crossing her cheeks.

"Have a good day, Sandy. When you're done here, why don't you go down to the beach and have a sno-cone."

He didn't look back. He took his camera, which he knew was almost new and cost in excess of $1,200.00 with all of the accessories. It was the best camera he'd ever owned.

Wait'll he told his Jean about his good fortune.

She'd die.

*****

30

"How long we holding this piece of shit?" asked the Lee County Medical Examiner, Peter Hillman, staring down at the blue-ish corpse with the jagged, Y-incision on his chest and abdomen.

"As long as it takes," said the 32-year-old Cape Coral Police Chief, Wayne Olsen. He was a big man with thinning hair and a no-nonsense tone. He could be imposing one moment and have you in stitches the next. "We got three more girls in the Cape we think are tied to him. Fort Myers has another two. Could be more."

"Like I said," said Hillman. "Piece of shit."

"Now he's rotting shit." said Olsen. "Keep him on ice and we'll burn him when everyone's done with him. We'll light cigars on his fuckin' flame. How's that work for you, sweetheart?"

"Works for me," said Hillman, sliding the drawer back into the refrigeration unit. "It's not like we don't have vacancies."

"We'll see if we can't do something about the lack of dead bodies," said Olsen, slapping him on the back. "You're all done with the autopsy and stuff?"

"Toxicology is still out. Someone calls every day, telling me to check for this or that. I see this dead prick more than I do my Tina."

"Let's hope he's more frigid," said Wayne, with a wink.

"Fuck you, Olsen."

"Not on your life, Pete. Talk to you later."

*****

31

Irv hadn't used the converted closet darkroom for a long, long time. He stopped by JH Camera and picked up a full darkroom kit by Beseler that only set him back around a hundred bucks. That, plus the cost of the camera, and he was still up a grand.

Irv was never that serious about photography, but he always thought that might be because he never wanted to fork out the bucks for a top quality camera. Now it had basically fallen into his lap.

He had no idea whether the developing chemicals he still had were subject to a shelf life, but there was no sense in wasting film, and the darkroom kit had everything he needed.

Irv was especially curious to see what was on the film left inside the camera. Not that he really gave a shit, but if there were any pictures of Richardson in there, he might make the effort to return them to the family. It would be a nice gesture. Hell, he'd give them his card too. Never know when someone might need a criminal attorney. This would definitely give them a reason to remember him.

Hell, maybe there was a shot of the killer. If that was the case, he could sell the pictures to the National Enquirer. Or maybe the headline could be, LAST PHOTOGRAPHS TAKEN BY MURDER VICTIM.

Irv got home and kissed Jean, his petite, put-upon wife, on the forehead. "I'll eat something later. Gonna develop some film."

"Some what?" she asked.

Irv did not answer. He went into the spare bedroom, which served as his office, and into the closet. He closed the door.

*****

The negatives looked promising. Irv could see the images there, and some of them were interesting. He completed the process. There had been nine photographs taken on the partially exposed roll of black and white film. All of them appeared to be of trees or a park at night.

The last one was a car. He could not see it clearly enough at the moment to tell what make or model, or really any detail. Maybe after he had them printed.

He did his test strips and noticed something strange about the park pictures. A black area, smack dab in the middle. It was a narrow test strip, so without the additional perspective, Irv had no idea what the blank space represented.

"Irv, you coming out for dinner?" asked Jean through the door.

"In a bit, sweetheart. Give me another half hour. And for God's sake, don't open the door."

He could hear the kids at the table, arguing over the vegetable Jean had selected for the night's dinner. He was glad to stay secluded in the darkroom for as long as possible.

Irv glanced up at his safe light, then back down at his work.

*****

The photos hung from the clips on the wire over his head. The image of the car came out perfectly. All of the others had a large, black space right in the middle. In the images where the zoom lens had clearly been in use, the space was wider and taller. In the images that were farther away, it was narrower and shorter.

But it looked like the outline of a man's figure. Somebody, anyway. The killer, perhaps?

The park looked familiar. Irv wondered if it had been Jaycee Park, right at the end of Beach Parkway where Richardson's house had been.

Irv shook his head. The car appeared sharp enough, as did everything except the one black space in each image. The photographs of the park were actually quite well shot, and with the lights reflecting off the river in the distance, it confirmed Jaycee Park had been the location.

"Well, shit," he said, plucking down the photographs one at a time and wadding them up along with the negatives. He took them to the trashcan and dropped them in, remembering it was trash day the following morning.

"I'm going to haul this trash out before dinner, honey," he said.

Irv made the rounds to the various trashcans throughout the house and took it all outside, filling the single, large can.

He opened the garage door and lit a cigarette. Jean would keep dinner hot for him, he knew. He held the smoke between his lips and tried to press the lid down on the metal can, but it was bent from past abuses by the waste disposal crew. He threw it aside and carried the can to the street.

As he put it down, he knocked the cherry off the tip of his Winston, and it dropped inside the trash can, unnoticed by Irv.

*****

As Irvin Wilford enjoyed his dinner, the contents of the garbage can ignited, shooting flames three feet in the air within another thirty minutes.

Alerted by his neighbors, Irv went out, saw the bonfire at the street, and ran to grab the garden hose.

He had no way of knowing that his carelessness had saved the lives of everyone in his family.

*****

CHAPTER ONE

Twenty Years Later – 2014:

Jack Hunger wasn't bored with his job. It was the only thing that really interested him. He lived in the small waterfront town of Cape Coral, Florida and worked for Lee County as a forensic photographer. He could be anywhere he was needed within an hour.

Crime wasn't so thick in the area that he was swamped. When he wasn't shooting actual crime scenes, he was analyzing images taken in extreme magnification to see if some clue or detail had been overlooked. That part of the job was tedious, but could be interesting.

Jack was only thirty-one years old, but he felt sixty-one. His ex-girlfriend, Debra, had left him a year before and moved to Pennsylvania.

Jack scrolled down the page and a picture came into view. It showed Debra and Peter Scranton, an upstart politician currently running for the Pennsylvania State Senate. She hung off his arm with a smile bigger than any Jack had ever witnessed in person. His eyes shifted to the politician.

His fucking teeth are perfect, thought Jack, bitterly.

Not that Jack's teeth were bad. It was just something to be pissed off about and it would do for now.

In fact, Jack knew it wasn't his looks that drove Debra away; he was 6'3", fluctuating between 210 and 215 pounds, and his chiseled, angular face and blue eyes were often the embarrassing conversation down at The Cop Shop, a local Cape bar. His hair was on the longer side, parted on the left and always neatly trimmed.

Jack Hunger could have brought a woman home most any night he went to The Cop Shop, but he realized that since Debra left, he'd pretty much been holing up at home more and more. His buddies tried to get him out, but he wasn't in the mood and there didn't seem to be any point.

Plus, there was – or might be – Hannah Maruska.

He stared at the screen for too long. Scranton was a good-looking enough guy, but reading about him, it seemed he didn't so much have policy positions, but instead, promised freebies to every constituent who voted for him. He seemed to think that once he was elected he would have a personal banking institution with unlimited funds available to him.

Jack released the mouse with more force than he intended, and it hit the cup of coffee sitting beside his monitor and sent it tumbling onto its side. There had been only two sips left in it, but it was enough to splatter his papers and make a fucking mess.

"For fuck's sake," he mumbled.

"What's wrong, Hunger?" asked Phil Eppler, the detective whose desk was just outside his office.

Jack shook his head. "Never mind. I'm done. I guess housekeeping'll clean this crap up."

"Don't count on it," said Phil, a balding detective near retirement. "I've had this chunk of bagel on the corner of my desk for like eight months. Looks like some mouse almost has it finished, but I ain't movin' it. Someday I'll complain."

"You'll be retired before then," said Jack. "See you tomorrow."

"Not if I see you first," said Eppler.

*****

It was only two o'clock, but the work was done and with his independent contractor status, Jack could come and go as he pleased. He was never truly off the clock; if someone needed a crime scene shot, he would be there when called, no matter what the hour.

It was important to get to a scene quickly, because greenhorn cops, dogs, parrots and kids could all screw up a crime scene in a myriad of ways. Jack had seen it all, and he was the best. There were others who could be called in an emergency, but Jack Hunger is who most detectives preferred.

As he drove, Jack eyed the glove box. There was a pack of smokes in there; a stale pack of Marlboro reds that he'd bought six months earlier. Five were gone.

It was time for six, so he leaned over and opened the box, removing the pack. He smoked one a month. It was his compromise. He had once smoked a pack every couple of weeks, but that was one of the excuses Debra used when she left him.

She pretended to be into fitness, but Jack had never seen her so much as do a sit-up. She faithfully wore the workout clothes, but Jack knew she didn't have a gym membership, so it was all for show.

So, while Jack knew her blaming his smoking was bullshit, he also knew it wasn't good for him. Now his plan was to buy a pack, smoke one each month, and by the time he got to the last one, a little over a year from now, it would be so stale and harsh he would just quit forever.

He unrolled all four windows and lit the smoke. As be breathed in the first hit, the nicotine rush was instantaneous. He'd tried the vapor cigs. It just wasn't enough. Nothing replaced the taste and high of an infrequent Marlboro.

Driving south down US 41, also known as Tamiami Trail, named so because it ran between Tampa and Miami, he noticed a new store had gone in where the old book store had been.

"Fuck!" he said, blowing out the smoke, staring at the new store's sign. "Seriously?"

The book store where he got all of his used paperbacks was gone, and a new thrift store had a GRAND OPENING banner over the door.

Jack shook his head. "Perfect," he said.

The Rolling Ladder had been an odd name for a bookstore, but it was explained the moment you saw the floor to ceiling shelves and the ornate, antique ladder that rolled along the length of the floor all day.

After Debra had left, he had turned to reading to pass the time. Not new literature; mostly his old favorites that he hadn't read since he was a kid. King's The Stand, Koontz's Watchers, Richard Adams' Watership Down and Whitley Streiber's The Wolfen.

It had been the last store in town besides Books-A-Million and Barnes & Noble. Neither of the big box stores sold used paperbacks, so maybe it was time to get a new hobby. Fuck it.

Suddenly, Jack wondered if the bookstore had donated any of its huge stock to the new thrift store. It *was* possible, maybe even likely. He put on his blinker and cut into the right lane, then swung his black 2012 Camaro into the parking lot.

He got out and went inside the store. The brass bell over the door tinkled and a pleasant, older woman whose name tag said Lilly approached him. "Welcome to The Good Stuff," she said. "Lots of merchandise and excellent prices. We just opened this morning."

"Hello," said Jack. "The Good Stuff, huh?"

"We think so," said Lilly. "Everything in this store has been tested and it all works as advertised. Lots of folks coming in to tell me how upset they were at the bookstore being closed."

"Yeah, I was disappointed, to be honest. I used to come to Rolling Ladder a lot."

"So did I," Lilly said. "It's how I got the job. I came here to buy a book and saw it was gone."

"Did they buy any of their stock? Any of the books?" asked Jack.

"Very good question," said Lilly. She was a very thin, petite woman, probably in her mid-seventies. Her smile was infectious and she used it constantly. "The answer is no. The owners decided to move the entire operation up to Pittsburgh."

Fucking Pennsylvania again, thought Jack. *I'll bet the store is walking distance from Debra and Peter's place. Bitch has never read a goddamned book in her life.*

He took a deep breath.

"Something wrong?" asked Lilly.

Jack shook his head. "No. I'm just going to look around then."

"Call if you need help."

"I will."

He moved down the aisle. Blenders, toasters, can openers. In the kitchen aisle. At least it was organized.

He moved down each aisle, seeing good prices hand-marked on tags hanging from things for which Jack had no need.

The next aisle was crammed with various electronics. CD and DVD players, old tape recorders, princess telephones, rotary telephones like the ones he'd seen in old movies.

Jack turned down and perused the shelves, moving things around to see items tucked in the back of the deep racks. There was a lot of inventory.

He slid aside a Westinghouse alarm clock to reveal a camera. It appeared to be a 35mm Pentax K1000 with a 50mm lens attached. He reached in and picked it up.

Jack had wanted a camera like that one since he was nine years old. He'd always admired the photographers at ball games and other sporting events, their foot-long-

41

plus lenses trained on the players, stopping the action with high-speed film.

He turned the camera over in his hands. It was in great shape. A couple of dings on the body, but only a couple. Almost no scratches, either. He saw the tag and turned it over.

$25.00 w/lenses, it read.

Lenses. Jack quickly slid the Westinghouse clock further aside and moved an old Brownie hand-wound movie camera to the right and saw a leather camera bag in the back. He bent down, put the camera on the floor and moved some more items to enable him to slide the case from the shelf.

It was in crap shape. He flipped the satchel flap and pulled the bag open. Inside was a 6-inch long, Sigma 70-210mm zoom lens that looked as pristine as the camera itself.

He retrieved the Pentax from the floor, dropped it into the bag and closed it, carrying it all up to the front desk.

"Find everything alright?" asked Lilly, still smiling. She twirled her dyed, blonde hair around a finger.

"Absolutely. The tag says this camera and the lenses are $25.00. Is that correct?" He put the bag on the counter in front of her.

She opened the flap and removed the camera, looking at the tag. Jack watched her, hoping her fingers did not weaken momentarily. The camera was older and heavier than modern cameras. He estimated the age of this one at around twenty five years, but he could not be sure without searching the serial number on the internet.

She put the camera back into the bag and looked up at Jack, nodding and smiling. "That's right. I suppose the kids all use their phones to take pictures nowadays. Owners must've figured nobody wants this old junk anymore."

Jack's disappointment over the missing bookstore had completely dissipated. His mind spun at what his next step would be. He was genuinely excited for the first time in months.

"You're in Florida," she added. "Got a sportsman's case over there, supposed to fit 35 millimeter cameras."

"What's that?"

"Waterproof case," she said. "If you get caught in the rain, good thing to have with you."

"How much?" Jack turned to look toward the aisle.

"Hold on." She walked quickly to the aisle and was back in less than thirty seconds with a faded box in her hands. "This case is actually new," she said. "Plastic jobbie with an o-ring seal and a snap latch. Some guy brought in like five of them. This is the last one. Five dollars."

"Ring it up," said Jack.

*****

By the time he got out of the thrift store it was 3:00 PM. He turned right on US 41 and headed to Ritz Camera at the Edison Mall, hoping to find film and a simple darkroom kit.

No darkroom supplies at all. Not even any film cameras in stock except a small selection of disposable cameras everyone used to use at weddings before the era of the camera phone. They did have 100, 200 and 400 ISO black and white film, so Jack bought five rolls of each.

Still, he wanted to develop it himself; that was part of the intrigue of this whole photography kick he intended to get on. So, even with his bag of film, Jack walked out of the store disheartened. Instead of trying elsewhere, he drove home, hoping to catch Hannah before she left for the day.

Hannah Maruska was the woman who cleaned his home weekly. It was not a large house; a two bedroom home located in an older area of southeast Cape Coral. The area was called The Yacht Club, and while the home was on a canal with access to the Gulf of Mexico, it was not nearly as prestigious as some might imagine from hearing the name. The homes there were mostly built in the 1960s and 1970s, little concrete block cubes with the waterfront being the most expensive feature.

Hannah was sweet and soft-spoken, but she was also beautiful. When her mouth was closed or she was listening to something Jack was telling her, her green eyes sparkled with interest. When she opened her mouth to smile or laugh, she beamed. Jack would give anything to kiss her just at those moments.

Was she just being polite, or was that interest real, and possibly directed at more than the things he said? Jack wondered. He sometimes wished. If he were honest with himself, it was more than sometimes, but the last thing he wanted to do was to frighten her away. He would rather worship her without her knowledge than lose her.

He pulled up and parked – there was no garage – and went toward the house, stopping on the porch to do his best to straighten his hair. He tucked in his shirt, too. He had packed on twenty pounds during the last months with Debra, eating out of depression for what he knew was to come. Luckily, he'd lost a lot of that weight after Debra left him, and that made his time spent at the gym less grueling. The flab firmed up and he retired a lot of his old clothing.

Sometimes he wondered if he didn't do all of it for Hannah. No matter. Three times a week at the Health and Strength Gym was good for him.

When he felt he was somewhat presentable, he went inside the house. The door was open and he heard Bad Company on the stereo. Hannah's favorite. She was only twenty-six years old, but some how Ready For Love was her favorite tune.

"Jack," she said, smiling as he came in the door.

He had been watching her before he opened the screen door, bending over with her dust rag, lifting items from the table and cleaning beneath them, shaking her butt to Rock Steady, another of their greatest hits.

"Hey, Hannah," he said, returning her smile. "Wrapping it up?"

"I was a little late getting here, so I have about a half hour to go," she said, her Czech accent pronounced. "When the clothes are done, I will get them folded and put away, and that's it."

"Take your time," he said waving her off. "You're not interrupting anything, trust me."

The 50" television was turned on with the sound down. As he glanced at the screen, he saw a banner at

the bottom that read: BREAKING NEWS –
SUSPECTED PRISON ESCAPEE TRAPPED IN FORT
MYERS HOME.

Jack went to the coffee table and grabbed the
remote, powering off the CD and turning the sound up on
the television. "Sorry to do this, Han, but something's
going on." He nodded toward the TV.

"Wow," she said. "What escapee? From where?"

"Two guys escaped from the federal prison in
Coleman, up in Sumter County," he said. "One was
found dead two days later, but the other's still on the run.
Might be him. Sergei Veselov."

"Russian?" she asked, standing beside the sofa
looking at him with her soft, green eyes and upturned
nose.

Jack lost his train of thought for a moment, but
answered. "Uh ... yeah, Russian mafia guy."

Hannah, who was about 5'5" tall with creamy skin
and long, petite fingers, sat down on the sofa beside him,
staring at the TV screen. Jack scooted a bit to give her
room, but not too much. He liked her closeness.

The reporter in the background stood in front of
several police cars behind him that sat parked bumper-to-
bumper, sealing off the area. The officers were unrolling
crime scene tape as he spoke:

"The prisoner that escaped with a fellow inmate
from the federal correctional complex in Coleman,
Florida last Tuesday is believed to be inside the home
behind me."

Jack squinted at the screen. "That house is in
Lehigh Acres, not Fort Myers."

46

"I hope it's not near my house," said Hannah. "And if it's him, I hope they catch him."

"If it's him, I'd strongly recommend he surrender."

"Do you think he will?"

"Idiots will be idiots. I doubt it."

"What was he in prison for?" she asked.

"He was a meth dealer," said Jack. "Got into a turf war with another head honcho, so he tracked down the guy's family and killed every last one of them. His parents, sister, two brothers and his twin boys."

"Oh, my God," said Hannah, her hand over her mouth. "How old were the twins?"

Jack looked at her and had a strong impulse to kiss her. She had never showed any interest in him that he'd noticed. He pushed the idea out of his mind.

"They were six years old," he said. "I know it's terrible, but their daddy was in the wrong business. He brought that crap down on his family, and it wasn't all that much of a surprise to the folks who know that world."

"But still," said Hannah. "The poor children. I hope they did not suffer."

Jack shook his head, but didn't answer, taking it as a rhetorical sentiment. The truth was, he'd never tell Hannah how the kids had died.

Veselov's claim to fame was dismembering people with his bare hands, and he did it while they were still alive, beginning with the extremities. It was the exact method used on the six-year-olds.

The Russian was over 6'7" tall and as strong as the proverbial ox. According to autopsy reports, Veselov broke the bones with brute force, bending the extremities as far in the wrong direction as possible. Then, with his enormous hands, Sergei would grip the skin and twist, standing on top of the body if necessary to get the leverage and grasp needed.

Veselov would then twist and pull until the arm or leg tore off. Sometimes there was evidence of him using a blade of some kind, but it was always clear when it was Veselov's handiwork.

If the victim was unlucky enough to live after their first arm had been ripped off, the Russian had been known to beat them with the severed limb to wake them if they passed out before he was finished.

The horrific, bloody scenes where Sergei had wreaked his revenge were often puke fests for the first officers to arrive. Nobody could prepare themselves for brutality like that.

Thankfully, the killer had never ventured this far south in Florida – at least until now. And the fellow escapee who had been found dead? He had been discovered torn apart in a vacant Tampa duplex.

Sure, the kids suffered, thought Jack. The Russian thug's modus operandi was maximum pain infliction. It did not matter whether it was a child, a woman or the man who had been the source of the perceived offense against Veselov.

The thoughts rolled through Jack Hunger's mind like a documentary film reel. Sergei Veselov was perhaps the most dangerous criminal housed in Florida's prison system.

"I'm pretty sure the kids never knew what hit 'em," said Jack, patting her knee.

She shook her head and put her hand over his for a brief moment before allowing her soft fingers to slide off.

Jack wondered if he'd imagined them lingering there for just an additional fraction of a second.

"They're ordering us to move away from the house now," said the reporter. "We're going to attempt to get our cameras in an elevated position to the north of the home and get a clear view of the scene from a safer location. Back to you in the studio for now."

The buzzer sounded on the clothes dryer, causing both Jack and Hannah to jump. They both laughed.

"Looks like I might be busy tonight if this goes wrong," said Jack.

"I'm sorry," said Hannah. "I know you need down time."

"It's my job, Han. Glad to have it in this economy."

"As am I," she said. "I'll get those clothes folded and get out of your way."

"Like I said, you're no bother. You're welcome to stay over and have a can of chili with me for dinner."

"I do like chili," she said.

*****

The news reporter had apparently worked his magic with a neighbor two streets over, for he now stood on the upper balcony of a two-story home and their powerful zoom camera lens showed the front door of the house surrounded by police.

It was like standing in the front yard.

"I can't believe this," said Hannah. "I'm almost afraid of something happening. I don't want to see it so clear."

She took a bite of chili as they sat side-by-side on the couch. He had gotten both of them Miller Lites, which now stood sweating on the glass table in front of them with no coasters.

"You don't wanna see it because you got a good heart and you don't like to see people suffer."

"So do you, Jack."

He shrugged. "Cops pretty much expect bad things to happen I think," he said. "I think we get a little surprised when it doesn't, sometimes."

"Maybe you have to say those things to make your police friends think you're tough," she said, smiling. "But you are a nice man, Jack."

"Holy shit," said Jack, finishing a swig off his beer.

As a young police officer had stood on the front stoop staying against the wall of the covered porch, the door flew open hard, slamming into the cop.

Nobody was visible in the open doorway, and after hitting the officer, it swung closed again. The unconscious man fell forward, landing face down. He didn't move.

"Jesus, that kid is hurt," said Jack, standing up, his eyes glued to the images. "Entry doors are solid in Florida."

As they watched, two officers trotted across the street in a crouched position, but the door opened two feet and the cop's body began to move. In a swift motion, he was dragged into the house and the door again slammed closed.

"Fuck!" shouted Jack.

Hannah stood and took his hand, squeezing it. "Jack, is there something you need to do? I can go."

"I'm not very good company, that's for sure," he said. "Yeah, Han. I'm sorry. I don't think this is going to end well. You'd better go."

She started to clear the dishes and he held her wrist gently with his hand. "No, no. I'll clean this up. You go on home. Thanks for staying a while. I really enjoy spending time with you."

She looked at the screen one last time, then back at him. She tiptoed and kissed him on the cheek, her lips just touching the corner of his mouth.

"I'll see you next week." Her eyes took on a hint of sadness.

"Hannah," he said. "Maybe … well … you still going to night school?"

"Three nights a week," she said. "Not on Tuesdays and Thursdays, and not on the weekends."

"Maybe I can take you for something better than chili one night. You know, like out on a date or something."

"That would be nice," she said, her mood brightening noticeably as a smile touched her lips. "I would enjoy that."

"Okay, then," said Jack, pulling open the door. She walked outside, turned again and gave him a wave.

Behind him the reporter said, "Cut the camera, Phil!"

When he jerked around to see what had happened, the image had returned to the newsroom and the anchor's face had gone white.

When he turned back, Hannah was gone.

He went back and sat on the couch. The news anchor did not replay any video, nor did she say what had just happened.

Jack called the station.

*****

Jack had his work bag locked in the trunk of his car, but he emptied everything out of the Pentax bag and just took the camera, the lenses and two rolls of each speed of film.

What he stood to photograph would not be pretty. As he had suspected, it ended very badly. A rookie cop was dead and the Russian had died in a barrage of SWAT gunfire.

Jack felt nervous. He rubbed his neck as he turned left on Veterans Parkway toward the Midpoint Bridge. Traffic was pretty light, so he didn't bother with the lights.

He had been right; the house wasn't in Fort Myers, but it was close. It was just off Lee Boulevard in Lehigh Acres, off Gunnery Street. The house was on Gordon Avenue South.

When Jack pulled up there were so many cars he couldn't see the house. He parked in a vacant lot across the street, practically finding the last available patch of grass in which to park, and grabbed his digital camera, which he hung from the strap around his neck, and threw the Pentax bag's strap over his shoulder.

The officers looked grim. It was for good reason, but Jack didn't know how true the words were until he stepped inside the house.

Plastic barricade sheeting had been pulled across the porch and outside the front windows of the house. When Jack walked up to it and looked over, he knew why.

A severed arm lay on the porch, the attached hand facing palm up. It had clearly been torn off the young officer. Jack powered on his camera and took several shots. He did not use the Pentax. It never crossed his mind. This was potentially one of the worst scenes of pure savagery he had ever witnessed.

"It ain't nice in there, Hunger," said his friend Nathan Dyer, a cop just two years from retirement.

Jack looked at him. "I get that, if this is any indication."

Nathan's eyes were sunken and tired. His hair, almost pitch black when Jack met him, was snow white. He walked with a slouch and just plain looked tired. The veteran cop was only forty-four, but he'd worked gang detail for much of his career, and had dealt with the worst in Lee County.

"This shit coulda waited until I was off the force. You'd have got no complaint from me."

Jack nodded. "It'll be over for you soon, Nate."

"Not fuckin' soon enough," he said, his face grim.

Nodding, Jack returned to a plastic chair set up in the driveway beside a table. There, he put on sterile gloves and shoe covers, and returned to the porch. There were corrugated steel hurricane panels mounted over all of the front windows, but in the center, two of the panels were missing, creating a gap of around 22". The glass was broken here. Jack nodded at Officer Dyer.

Dyer pulled back the barricade and he stepped inside, careful to avoid the blood spatter, which was in a straight line with the severed arm of the rookie cop. Tendrils lay bloodless and flattened, stuck to the concrete, stringing off the torn end of the extremity that had been ripped away from the shoulder socket.

"Guess you already know the arm belongs to Justin Sims," said Dyer. "Been with the department six months. Has a pregnant wife and a two-year-old girl at home."

"I called in," said Jack. "I know." He patted Dyer's arm as he went by.

Jack moved inside and immediately cringed. There were body parts and blood everywhere. "Careful to keep your eyes down," said Nate from behind him. "Watch your step. Olsen'll have a shit fit if we fuck up this crime scene."

52-year-old Wayne Olsen had to the position of Lee County Sheriff ten years earlier, after nearly sixteen years of service, part of which he served as Chief of Police in Cape Coral.

Jack wasn't too worried. When Jack was a twenty-one year old rookie, Wayne had taken over; despite their age difference, they got along well. Olsen seemed to take on a mentor role at first, but as time had passed, the men found they just enjoyed hanging out.

Over the years prior to his becoming sheriff, Wayne had been involved in a number of high profile cases in the past and one thing he did not tolerate was sloppy police work. Everyone knew it and acted accordingly.

Moving carefully, Jack stepped deeper into the house. The officers had set up lights on stands to illuminate the crime scene, as night had now fallen.

The young officer's torso, with only a single leg remaining, lay facing upward on the floor just six feet inside the room. The right leg had been broken already and twisted, so the only way to be sure the torso was on its back was the uniform itself. It had been torn open in the front, but the bright, star-shaped badge was there.

Another arm lay on the ground beside a wall that appeared to have been intentionally emptied of pictures and art. Jack looked behind him and saw several frames with shattered glass on the floor and on the sofa.

On the wall, at least two feet tall and six feet wide, it said, "DIE TIN MAN." It had clearly been marked there using blood smeared from the severed arm, like a giant Sharpie.

The words smeared on the wall weren't foreign to Jack. *Tin man.* It was what some criminals called cops, because of their badges. The young tin man on the floor had died a horrible death.

"The guy's dead, right?" asked Jack.

"Him?" asked Nate, looking at the body on the floor.

Jack looked at Nate. "Seriously? The fuckin' perp, Nate."

"Yeah, yeah. Sorry. He's dead. Real dead."

Jack didn't have to ask where they were because the shadows danced on the wall just outside a door in the back corner of the room.

Another officer stuck his head out of the room, lowered his filter mask and took a deep breath. He looked up and nodded to Jack.

"Hey, Hunger. You gonna shoot it now?"

"I've got enough to do here for a few. You need more time in there?"

"Yeah. Got a guy hurt in here and medics are working on him."

"Who?"

"Eddy. You know him."

"Yeah," said Jack. "He okay?"

"He'll be okay. Derek Williams saved him; fired the kill shot. Guy's a hero."

"Good. Get them outta there as soon as you can and for God's sake, don't touch anything."

"You got it," said the detectives, returning to what appeared to be a bedroom.

Jack turned back to look at Nate, who again stood in the doorway. "Where's his head?" asked Jack.

Nathan walked inside and slid between the loveseat and the corner table. He stared out the window toward the ground.

Jack walked and stood beside him.

Sheer curtains hung off a rod overhead, and a bloodstain decorated it at about shoulder height. Nate parted the sheers.

Jack looked down. The glass was broken out and the young officer's head lay in the dirt just outside the window. His eyes stared straight up, sightless and fixed.

"Holy Jesus," said Jack, though he was not religious. His Uncle Vince used to say that all the time and it stuck.

"Jesus had nothin' to do with this, Hunger. Better get shootin' or you'll be here all night. Let me know what you need."

Nate always helped out at crime scenes. Moving furniture out of the way so he could get better access to take the photographs, things like that. He wasn't afraid of hard work, but clearly he wanted to be done with it and retired already.

He shot photographs of the officer's severed head, then went outside to get closer. He knelt down and focused on the neck, snapping several pictures. Afterward, he covered it with a small tarp and went back inside.

"Where's his left leg?" he asked, looking around.

"It's in with him," said Nate. "You're on your own. Not goin' back in there."

Jack shook his head. "Where does filth like this come from, man?"

"Hell," said Nathan Dyer. "Straight from hell."

"He's back there now," said Jack. "Too late for this kid, but he got some instant justice."

"Ain't gonna do much to comfort his wife and kid."

Jack nodded his head. "Not to mention the one to be born without a dad." He shot photograph after photograph. A bloody knife lay on the floor next to the television.

Jack knelt down beside the torso and leg, shooting close-up images of the place the left leg once was. The knife had been used there. Apparently he was strong, but not quite enough to rip a man's leg off. Especially a young man with good muscle tone.

Fifteen minutes later, Jack had shot the scene in the front room. Now it was time to visit the place of the brutal killer's demise – the master bedroom.

*****

The home was clearly the winter home of a snowbird, the name for a person who only spent winters in Florida. The rear, roll-down hurricane panels were closed, and all of the side window panels were up, too. Veselov probably removed the two front panels so he'd have daylight inside. The power to the home was not working, probably because of nonpayment of a Lee County Electric Co-op bill.

Generators ran noisily outside and the light stands threw crazy shadows on the blood-spattered walls as Jack removed the Pentax from the bag and loaded it with 400 ISO film and tucked it back inside its case.

He would shoot everything he needed for work with his digital camera before using the Pentax to begin his photographic diary of the worst things cops might face on any given day.

When he entered the room, he saw Veselov immediately, but half of his right cheek was missing just below the eye socket, the bone there shattered. There was an enormous wound in his chest, and his gut looked as though it had exploded.

"Holy shit," said Jack. "Where'd you shoot him from?"

"Sig Sauer 556 handiwork," said the police sniper, Derek Williams, holding up the rifle. "We weren't taking any chances. Got him from the family room when he walked in front of the door. Five quick shots. Kept nailing him as he fell."

In the corner, another cop sat on a chair and two medics crouched beside him. Jack recognized him as a 10-year, veteran cop named Eddy Dempsey. He still had a full head of red hair and a freckled face that gave him a boyish look.

"Hey Eddy, you alright?"

"Thanks to Derek there, I sure am," he said, trying to force a smile and failing miserably. "I followed protocol, came in the room and that dead fuck there hit me with ... well ... let's just say he hit me."

"Is that your blood?" asked Jack. It was all over Dempsey's face and neck, the dark spots dotting his uniform, too. The medics were tending to his nose, and his eyes looked swollen. "Jeez, Eddy. You sure you're alright?"

He nodded. "I'm as well as can be expected."

He stopped speaking, and his eyes fell to the floor, then to the wall. Tears ran down his face and he buried it in his hands.

Jack went over to him and the medics moved away. "Hey, Eddy, man, it's okay. C'mon, buddy."

"It's not my blood," choked Eddy through his sobs. "Not all of it, anyway." He raised his arm and pointed where he had been avoiding his eyes since Jack had entered the room.

Jack looked around and saw it. It was the rookie cop's left leg. It lay bent at the knee on the floor beside the door through which Jack had just entered.

"He swung the leg at you?"

Dempsey nodded. "Caught me square in the face. I went down and Williams was right behind me. He took the fucker out just after."

"Good," said Jack. "I gotta get to work. You guys about wrapped up?" he asked the paramedics.

They stood and helped Eddy to his feet. He tested his steadiness and said, "Can you walk?"

"Yeah, I can walk. I coulda walked twenty minutes ago, too."

"I'll call you later tonight, Eddy, to check on you."

"At least this case is open and closed," he said. "Perp's dead. We move on except for Justin and Victoria and their girl."

"Their two-year-old's name is Lindsay," said Jack. "Plus the one on the way. With the new baby coming, they're really gonna need some help."

"Lucky she has us then," said Dempsey. "See ya, Hunger. Good luck with this mess."

"Glad you're alright," said Jack.

A rookie cop stood watch at the door while Jack shot the scene from every possible angle. When he was done with the official photographs, he got his new Pentax from the case and removed the lens cap.

Watching the floor carefully so he did not smear any evidence, he knelt beside the enormous Russian's destroyed body and took several photographs on manual focus. He moved to a different angle and took several more. The next shots focused on the wounds. They would be tolerable to look at in black & white, maybe.

Then, reversing a decision he had made earlier, he took shots of all of Sims' body parts. Different angles, nothing omitted. He wasn't sure he would do anything with them, but he had them.

It was 9:00 PM by the time he left for the evening. He would check online for the darkroom kit and maybe a book on photography and developing.

*****

CHAPTER TWO

*****

After he got home the evening of the killing of Sergei Veselov, Jack Hunger couldn't sleep.

He thought about Officer Sims and his family, and the horror his wife would experience when the officers showed up on her doorstep without her husband.

Sometimes Jack was glad he didn't have anyone. If things were to go south for him, nobody would care. His mother was dead and his father, a long-time cop, had left his mom and moved to Arizona when he was six. Today, as far as Jack knew, George Hunger was drowning in Jack Daniel's whiskey and self-pity.

That sleepless night, Jack went online and found a Beseler darkroom kit. It included an enlarger, paper, all the chemicals and the safe light.

With his Amazon Prime membership, the darkroom kit arrived on Friday, just two days after he shot the pictures. Jack had a small closet he wasn't using, so he tucked what was there into a corner and got a stool to stand on to replace the compact fluorescent bulb with the amber-colored safe light.

Saturday came, and he waited until the sun was up high enough that he could properly make the room lightproof. He went into the closet and closed the door. Ribbons of light shone in from all sides. He'd read on the internet the easiest way to eliminate all the light was to attach wide, felt strips to the door itself so that when it pulled closed, the felt would overlap the jamb and the hinge gap and seal everything out.

It took him all of thirty minutes to hot glue the felt on the door. When Jack went inside, it was pitch black.

He waited five minutes, allowing his eyes to adjust, and checked thoroughly.

Nothing. Done.

He tore the cellophane wrap off the instruction book and flipped through it to find the English instructions. Oddly enough, it was the third listed language after Spanish and French.

Next, he opened the door and prepared his table, which was a 4' wide camping table he'd picked up at Walmart. In the center of the table, he had cut out a 1' x 1' section and from the bottom, taped an opaque, white acrylic panel. Below this he mounted two small fluorescent light fixtures, effectively creating a light box for viewing negatives.

Jack placed the enlarger on the right side of the table, and used the existing closet shelf for the bottles of chemicals needed in the process. He could hang his negatives from the wire rack where many of Debra's clothes once hung.

After mixing up the appropriate amount of chemical for the film he would be developing, Jack closed the door, let his eyes adjust, and removed the film cartridge from the Pentax, setting the camera aside.

He pried the top off the canister with a church key can opener and removed the film within. From this point on, he knew that any screw-up on his part would ruin any chance of the images coming out. He thought back to the instructions and unrolled the film, running his fingers along the edges only. When he reached the end, he found the bend where it once hooked to the plastic roll, sandwiched in between his index and middle fingers, and snipped off the bent part with his scissors.

*****

The remainder of the process was tedious but exhilarating. When the negatives were completed, he could see the reverse image of the shots he had taken at the crime scene. They looked perfect.

Then something went wrong. Some of the images came out fine; others had a large, black spot, as though the negative was horribly underdeveloped. Jack picked up the negative strips and checked them.

Perfect. It was only on the developed pictures.

But not in all of them; only the images with bodies in them. The amber light glowing overhead, Jack stared at the newly developed photographs. If not for the blank spot, he would have been very proud of himself; the areas surrounding the spot were sharp and extremely detailed.

"Fuck me," said Jack. Not a single image of Sims had come out, nor had any of the Russian. Even in the photographs he'd taken of Sims' head, lying face-up in the garden outside the window, the photograph was perfect except for Sims' head. That was an oval, black spot.

Frustrated, Jack took the several photos with the blank spots and tossed them into the trash.

"Fuckin' Chinese film," he mumbled, re-inspecting the negatives. Yep. He could see the killer clearly, as well as the officer's body.

"What the fuck am I doing wrong?" he asked aloud.

Nobody answered his question, so he turned on the regular light and put everything away.

When he stepped out of the closet and looked at his watch, Jack was surprised to see it was dark outside.

Jack knew there was an alternate method to developing the film. He would use his scanner to produce them digitally.

But not tonight. It was only 9:00, but tonight he intended to pull American Graffiti from his DVD collection, slip back into the world of the early 1960s and drink a couple of beers. His new hobby had sapped him of quite enough energy for one night.

But he was encouraged. This was going to be fun.

And a fun distraction. He would try to get home early the next time Hannah was there, and shoot some random pictures of her. If he could take a very good one, he would frame it for her.

He'd keep one for himself, too. Seeing her once a week was beginning to not be nearly enough.

*****

11:15 PM
Medical Examiner's Office, Fort Myers, Florida

Kathryn Hightower was a workaholic. She had been Lee County's Medical Examiner since 2011, and the detectives liked her. She respected their investigations and preserved the deceased as evidence as long as she could.

Quite often, additional information could be gleaned from an intact corpse that could not be gotten after the autopsy. That is the very reason that as a rule, she would wait for three days before beginning the actual autopsy. The fluids were drawn and toxicology tests were ordered immediately, of course.

How the big Russian died was not in question; one look at the body and it was clear. No, it was how the man, even with his size, had possessed the energy and strength to dismember most of a human being with his bare hands.

She was of the initial opinion that the toxicology findings would indicate high levels of either PCP or meth, or some other adrenaline-pumping drug.

Kathryn ruled out bath salts; they tended to make a person temporarily insane and completely unaware of what they were doing; this killer had a plan, and that plan was to remove the officer's limbs one by one with sheer, brutal force.

The several pieces of the young police officer were currently stored in a single drawer behind her, laid out in the proper position, as though he would be sewn together and reconstructed.

Sergei Veselov lay on a table behind her. The bags had already been removed from his head, hands and feet, and all trace evidence had been removed and sent to the lab.

She recorded his name, gender, height, weight and age in her voice recorder. Next, she cut away his clothing and bagged it before inspecting his body for tattoos and other distinguishing marks. Using a magnifying glass, she made notes of each injury and mark on his skin. Turning the body was not possible tonight. She would do what she could, but would need help with this beast of a corpse tomorrow. The entire procedure could've waited, but Kathryn was dedicated and it had been a busy week of murders in Lee, Hendry and Glades Counties.

With regard to tattoos and marks, there were several to describe. She photographed each one as she went. Most were of symbols and obviously Russian language, the meaning of which she did not understand.

Next, she took his fingerprints and X-rayed all parts of his body, her intent to find any broken bones or other abnormalities. Hidden drugs had been located in this manner as well.

After taking a blood sample, Kathryn changed her apron from the sterile, white cloth version to one of rubberized material with a floral pattern; no sense in everything being utilitarian, particularly in a stainless steel and linoleum environment such as the one in which she spent much of her time.

She then washed the corpse thoroughly and patted it dry with disposable paper towels designed for the purpose, and put on a fresh pair of nitrile gloves. Of course, all the loose evidence had already been removed from the body and preserved, so there was no risk of losing anything critical to the investigation.

She lifted her dissecting knife from the table and extended the razor sharp, four-inch blade. As she moved to penetrate the skin, she looked up at the electric Westclox clock on the wall, its yellowed cord dangling down and inserted into the power outlet.

The clock had probably been in that room since Lawrence Kelly was the ME back in 1989. She noted the time. It had just turned 12:15 in the morning. Her husband and kids would be fast asleep now.

Daniel, Dan Jr. and Abigail were her entire world, but there were times and cases like that of Sergei Veselov that had the entire community in an uproar. They wanted to know how he escaped from the high security Florida prison.

The very fact is, they had not yet determined that. There were more Russian mafia types in that facility; if it happened once, it could happen again, especially if Veselov had conspired with others who had not broken out yet.

Once the story was out, citizens unfamiliar with Veselov's history would demand to know why the killer came to Lee County in the first place, and whom he had come to track down. Being unfamiliar with his modus operandi and brute strength, they might also suspect a new drug similar to bath salts had hit the streets.

They would not know that the Russian's ability to tear off limbs – an art perfected by Veselov over the years – was a result of practiced technique rather than drug-induced rage and power.

68

She began the initial cut, from neck to groin, diverting at the navel. It was necessary, for cutting through the navel was like trying to slice through leather with a butter knife.

When the cut was complete, Kathryn undercut the sheet of skin on the right side of the dead man's body; the left side was an enormous wound from multiple, high-caliber gunshot wounds. When she moved to fold that skin away, it detached in her hands and she placed it in a tray beside the autopsy table.

Next, she took another blood sample directly from the heart and put it aside. She made an incision in the bladder and collected a urine sample, which would be automatically tested for alcohol and metallic poisons.

As she leaned in to cut away the heart, something happened. A dark fluid began bubbling up from deep within the cavity of the body, as though coming from behind or under the corpse.

A finger on Veselov's right hand twitched and Kathryn screamed. She staggered backward and stumbled, slipping in water from the wash and landed on her backside.

Catching herself before hitting her head, the Medical Examiner stared toward the Russian's body. He lay still. She blinked her eyes and got back to her feet.

Kathryn didn't need someone coming in there and seeing her splayed out on the floor. It was not unheard of for detectives to drop in at any hour of the night for any number of reasons.

She brushed her apron down, checked herself, and moved back toward the table. Feeling a bit foolish, she reached down and tentatively took his wrist, feeling for a pulse.

Stop it, Kathryn. You're being stupid and acting like a little girl!

Her eyes moved back to the body cavity. Yes, the black liquid was still there. She lifted another syringe from the table and drew a sample. It was unlike anything she had ever seen come from a corpse. Perhaps it was the result of some contamination or poison with which she was not familiar.

A chill ran down her neck.

Poison. She had not considered it. It could be a toxin with no smell or taste. Or maybe she was just freaking herself out. Of course if it was anything like that, she would already be dead.

It was late. Kathryn decided she would finish some basic tests, put Veselov back in the drawer and finish tomorrow with fresh eyes and a regenerated mind, unsullied by hours of work.

She stepped to the top of the angled table and put a thumb on Veselov's eyelid, lifting it to inspect the conjunctivae on his eyes.

The pupil suddenly contracted to a fine point, and the other eye opened. Both stared at her and she screamed.

Before she could move away from the table, two tree stump arms jutted out toward her and powerful hands grabbed her neck. The body of Sergei Veselov opened his mouth to reveal inky blackness that ran and oozed from his parted lips, even as it began pouring from his nose, ears and eyes. He screamed, a deep, reverberating tone that might have come from Hell itself.

I'm going to die at the hands of a dead man, thought the M.E. It was the last thought Kathryn Hightower would ever experience.

She passed out from the pressure on her windpipe and never felt her head finally twist free of her neck and land hard against the linoleum floor.

*****

Sergei Veselov felt his power the moment he had his first conscious thought.

Whatever coursed through his veins was like the best cocaine or crystal he had ever had. He wanted to be moving the moment he awoke, but something told him the woman leaning over him would be a problem. She stared down at him, her eyes wide with shock, a scream caught in her throat.

He gripped her head and twisted it off, tearing the skin and snapping the spinal cord. His large hands performed the deed with the ease an angry child might experience while tearing the head off a least favorite doll. Sweet blood spewed from her neck and warmed his face and he . . .

. . . remembered. The young cop. He had first hit him with the door of the house he was hiding in. He still wasn't sure how.

He licked more of the blood from his lips and closed his eyes. It tasted sweet; like the breast milk he could somehow vividly recall from his infancy. He remembered reaching his little hands out before he could even walk, finding the soft flesh of his mother's bosoms, and suckling there until he fell asleep.

71

This was that powerful a draw.

He sat up and felt everything shift downward. Black liquid ran from the enormous opening in his chest and stomach. He eased his legs over the side of the table and sat there for a moment. With the damage done to his body, could he walk?

Being more careful than his condition indicated was necessary, even to him, he lowered his foot to the floor and stood on it, putting much of his weight there. He put the other foot down and walked, avoiding the blood of the woman in the apron.

Everything shifted again and the black, ink-like substance ran from his many wounds. He stopped and stared down at them. At his internal organs. He could not identify many of them, but his heart was there. It was not moving. He reached up and touched it with a tentative finger. Poked it. He felt nothing.

He then closed his hand around it and gently massaged it. He'd seen that on some television show; the doctor massaged the heart into beating once more.

Nothing. It was cold. Sergei moved his hand lower. Cold. Everything.

I'm dead, he thought. *Somehow, I'm dead and somehow I'm not.*

Now, some things were clear. At first he wasn't sure why the woman had been frightened. He had just woken up, and hadn't felt angry. It often took the stupidity of his comrades or the prison guards to draw his rage out of him, and that normally did not happen until at least after breakfast.

No, he did not realize the cause of her fear until she was already dead. That was when he looked down at his own chest and abdomen, realizing the impossible; he was dead, too. Either that or horribly wounded.

Only now he was awake and he felt no pain at all; only an unfamiliar power running through his veins. He had always felt strong because he was; this was different.

Sergei Veselov felt invincible.

Sergei continued to stare down at his opened body and bit by bit, it came back to him. He had been in a gun battle with police and SWAT. He had killed a young tin man.

Everything swam back into focus. The message he'd scribed on the wall with the dead cop's arm.

Die Tin Man.

He had known he did not stand a chance then; so what was he doing here now, sitting on a table in what looked like a ... a morgue?

A noise came from behind him. He listened and he was curious, but he found he could not focus on it. His eyes kept turning to the body of the woman he had killed moments before.

Sergei felt a hunger burning within him, and he stared at the woman's body, no longer seeing her as a victim or a corpse, but as ... meat. He felt himself drawn to her. Her flesh would still be tepid and sweet, so tender in his mouth.

He knew it should trouble him. He had never before wanted to eat his victims or anybody else. Something pulled him to her, though. Her body, when consumed, would fill and warm him.

Sergei Veselov, in his new, unfamiliar form with his new, unfamiliar desires, rushed to the stainless steel counter that ran from the door to the wall of drawers. He yanked open the drawers and tore through them, searching. When he opened the third drawer, he found what he wanted. Gauze, and lots of it. Ace Bandages, too.

Veselov tore open a pack of the gauze. He turned behind him and saw what appeared to be some of his skin on the stainless steel cart. He reached back and grabbed it, then placed it over his stomach where the missing skin was. He started the gauze and tried to wrap it around him.

The gauze sprung free. He tried again, reaching around his back as he attempted to wrap the gauze around his midsection. It sprung free again.

"Arghhhhhhh!" he screamed aloud in frustration. He searched the drawers again and found what appeared to be an industrial stapler. He knew what it was for; it was for sealing wounds and incisions. They still used stitches at the prison, but out in the everyday world they often used staplers.

He held the gauze in place and placed the stapler against it. He pulled the trigger and it clicked and vibrated in his hand.

I didn't feel anything, he thought. *I am dead.*

He looked down at his wound again, and at the long cut that ran from as high up as he could see to his abdomen. He put the stapler in his jaws and reached down to pull the skin flap on one side to meet the piece he had taken from the table. He stapled them together.

Next, he stapled the other end of the loose skin flap to his attached skin. It took nine staples to do it right. Then he stretched them together and attached them, continuing up his stomach and chest until he could no longer see the incision that had most likely been made by the dead woman on the floor … as part of what? His autopsy?

He searched the room and saw a door. He moved toward it and opened it.

A bathroom. A mirror. He turned on the light switch, leaving a black, inky stain on the wall. He looked in the mirror and put the staple to work on his chest, all the way up to his neck. When he was done he dropped the stapler in the sink and went back to the counter.

When he was all finished, Sergei's stomach and chest was mummified in Gauze. After that, he got the Ace Bandage and completed the wrap. Not too tight; he still needed mobility.

His eyes went to the woman's body again. Something within him cried out, demanding sustenance. He knew where his mind was venturing, but for some reason it did not bother him. It was exactly what he wanted. It was what he had to have. Meat. Her meat.

As a boy in Russia, Sergei never had enough food. He was lucky to have bread and milk and the occasional dried meat.

His mouth watered. He felt the liquid flowing over his tongue, but when he opened his mouth, only more of the inky black liquid poured out, running down his chin and staining the newly applied Ace Bandage.

Intact and feeling as though more of the black stuff would not spill out the moment he dropped, Sergei did just that. With both massive hands, he gripped the blouse of the dead woman and tore the material away as if it were pillow stuffing.

Her skin appeared, pale and white. He ran the palm of his hand over it, allowing the tips of his fingers and his fingernails to dig into it slightly, but not enough to break the skin.

He would break the skin, but not with a knife, nor with his fingers. When he did it, he wanted only one thing; for her blood, warm and thick, to wash into his mouth and satisfy his insatiable hunger.

He dropped his face down, his mouth stretched open. With a single close of the jaw, he clamped down, feeling his teeth sink into the flesh and meet, uppers to lowers. He tore the flesh away and chewed it; the taste was better than the sashimi he had once enjoyed at the high-end sushi restaurant in the Hotel Salut in Moscow.

Sergei found he could not be satisfied. With each bite and swallow, he felt power and a simile of life throbbing inside him. He ate until his desire passed.

The thump came from behind him once again.

This time, with a keen awareness of his surroundings and seemingly increased senses, he got back on his knees and threw a foot under him. He stood easily without supporting even a hand on a table.

Veselov went back into the bathroom and turned the light on again. He studied his face in the mirror, amazed. The right side of his cheek was gone, and the black liquid had stained much of his remaining skin. He turned on the water and tried to rinse the black away, but only the woman's blood ran into the sink. He noticed for the first time that his fingers and palms were also stained black from whatever the liquid was.

Sergei returned to the gauze drawer and opened a new roll. He pulled out a three foot long piece and balled it up, stuffing it in the wound on his cheek. Once it was in place, he searched and found the large wound self-adhesive bandages and tore open the box, taking one out.

Sergei went into the bathroom and stood before the mirror to apply the bandage. Maybe if any facial recognition software was in use in the hunt for him, that would help.

A muffled cry then came from behind him and he jerked toward it. Two more thumps.

He moved toward the wall of refrigerated drawers and listened as he walked back and forth. As he stared at drawer #2, located in the center of the first row of stainless steel drawer fronts, he heard the thump again. Veselov reached out and put a hand on it.

Thump. Thump. Another muffled cry; but one that sounded as though a man spoke through water and cloth.

He moved his hand toward the handle and grasped it. No fear touched his dead heart. Whatever was there, he would deal with it. He pulled it open, sliding it all the way out until it stopped and he could see the entire length of the black bag within.

He moved to the tag clipped to the zipper and read it.

Justin Sims.

The name was familiar. The name badge on the cop he'd killed said Sims.

He hadn't just killed him. Sergei smiled as he recalled tearing the man limb from limb, knowing it was his last act as a living human being. The Tin Man had died before Sergei had finished ripping off both arms.

He remembered watching the officer's eyes and the terror registered there, finally sinking to sightless nothings as he had written his message on the wall with blood utilized from Sims' severed arm. Prison was no longer an option. He had made the mistake of cooperating with a guard for extra privileges, and that had been discovered by other members of Krovozhadnost. The name translated to English in only one word: Bloodthirst.

Sergei watched the bag twitching and jerking and wondered if he was delaying the inevitable. If the cop was in this bag, he was in pieces. If the same thing had happened to the tin man as had happened to him, every little piece of him was alive.

*****

The next morning, Jack Hunger awoke from a fitful sleep. It was Sunday and there was no football this time of year, so that was not on the menu of things to do. Perhaps he would go see a movie. Or go take some more pictures and try to get them right this time.

Not bodies. Just birds and things. They would not go into the same scrapbook as his crime scene photographs, but he might frame them just to let Hannah know he did have a soft side.

Yeah, he thought. *I'll go get some color film and do my best to compose some pretty pictures for a change.*

He padded into the kitchen and put on the coffee, before grabbing the Pentax from the table. He sat down as the coffee pot spit and bubbled, turning the camera over in his hands.

Real clean for a twenty-year-old camera, he thought. *Thing'll be a collector's item one day.*

He looked up and his eye fell on the trashcan. One of the photographs he tossed was sticking out a bit, and he noticed a distinct absence of the black spot that had caused him to trash it in the first place.

He put the Pentax down and went to the wastebasket. He plucked the photograph out and saw that the one beneath it had somehow also developed. The killer's image was there. Clear as day.

"This makes no fuckin' sense," he said aloud.

Of course it didn't make sense. He'd put the photographs in the stop solution when the majority of the image was properly developed. Black spots and holes had flawed the photographs the night before, wherever bodies or body parts were.

Now there was Veselov, perfectly developed in the images.

He flipped through the other prints. The ones of the dead, dismembered officer had finished developing, too. Every image was perfect now.

Jack Hunger realized he had a lot to learn about photographic development.

A whole lot.

His phone rang. It was Sheriff Wayne Olsen. He had disturbing news.

*****

On the way to the morgue, Jack recounted the words the sheriff had used: *I don't know how to tell you this, Jack, but Kathryn Hightower's dead, and so is Ames, our night guard. I need you here like yesterday, and I don't want you saying a word to anyone.*

79

Jack had questions, none of which Wayne would answer. All of it was baffling and disturbing.

The last two things Wayne had told him had been delivered with great reluctance, and after hearing it, Jack had white-knuckled the phone, finding he had no words. He had no idea how to process the information, but one thing was certain; he was positive he had heard Wayne wrong.

Officer Sims, who had been decapitated and dismembered by Sergei Veselov, save for a single leg, was showing signs of life. Veselov was gone.

If the revelation about Officer Sims was true, it would not provide any relief or joy. The news could only instill terror to any whom had seen Sims' body.

Jack Hunger pressed his right foot on the accelerator of the Camaro, wanting more than anything in the world to turn around and go back home. He looked beside him on the seat. The Pentax was there, along with his regular camera and lenses.

He fought the urge to make a U-turn and drove on toward the county morgue.

*****

CHAPTER THREE

*****

The guard had disabled the emergency exit door alarm, most likely. He liked to smoke and often turned off the alarm and slipped out the rear door for a Marlboro. Nobody had reason to complain about it until now. Whoever had taken Veselov's body had left the building that way.

When the morning receptionist had arrived at work, she had found Paul Ames spread forward on his desk, arms out, palms flat on the desk – with his dead face staring at the ceiling. His neck was clearly broken.

It was a chain reaction of death.

Detectives determined that Nancy White had walked into the room and had seen Ames' body. Her purse was spilled out on the floor just inside the employee entrance.

She had apparently run from the building into the street, where she dialed 911 before dropping her phone in a panic. Nancy was then struck by a 34' RV as she bent over to retrieve her dropped phone. The front bumper of the RV hit her from behind, knocking her hard forward, causing her head to slam into the asphalt with extreme force, the blunt trauma killing her instantly, the undercarriage of the big RV twisting her body like a Twizzler.

The RV driver had dialed 911, and Sheriff Olsen arrived at exactly the same time as the EMS and police.

When Jack arrived, Wayne had the entire building sealed off.

Wayne had been standing outside, looking pale and unsure. Jack was concerned the moment he saw him.

"C'mon in," said Wayne, lifting the crime scene tape.

Jack ducked under and walked beside him as he hurried through the doors.

"Wait outside," he said to the group of officers who had been prepared to follow them inside.

"But Sheriff, we need –"

Olsen put a hand in the air. "You need to give us a few minutes. I'll call you back in when we're ready, but you're limited to the front. Stay out of the morgue and everywhere else in the building until I give you the go ahead. Got it?"

Nobody answered. It was clear that their Sheriff was upset and had made up his mind about it.

"Kathryn's back here," said Wayne, after they had cleared the earshot of the crowd. "On the floor of the autopsy room."

"Does anyone know about her yet?"

"No."

"Jesus, Wayne," said Jack. He did not call him Sheriff Olsen or sir when they were alone. Their ranks within the department and their age difference had become less and less of a factor over the years. They could not help but consider themselves friends first. "Where's the surveillance video?" asked Jack. "Let's look at it."

Olsen shook his head, looked unsure for a moment, then said, "It's already in the FBI's hands."

"The Feds? Why?"

"Veselov's gone," said Olsen, stopping in the hallway midway between the front room and the morgue.

"Wayne, what the hell happened here last night? Where's Veselov? Why the Feds?"

"I just told you," said Wayne. "Exactly *because* Veselov's gone, Jack. The Feds ... you know how they are. They wanted the body after Kathryn was finished with the autopsy, and they're pissed, first of all. They saw Veselov as their body. Now he's gone and you know how that goes."

"Okay, but what about the video showing what happened to Paul?"

Again, Olsen shook his head. "All of it. They got it." He would not look Jack in the eye.

"Well, did *you* see it first, anyway?" asked Jack.

Wayne did not answer the question. Jack stared at him for a moment. "Wayne?"

Something was very wrong with Olsen. He was a smartass and he was sometimes a prankster. Last, he was a damned good cop and a better Sheriff that all the cops respected, but he was never at a loss for words.

Jack reached down, grabbed Olsen's hand and held it up. It was trembling like a cold, newborn puppy.

"What the fuck's going on, Wayne? What was on that tape?"

Olsen started to shake his head again, but Jack put a hand on his shoulder. "No more stalling, man. I've known you too long for that kinda crap. Tell me what you saw."

Wayne's eyes met his. "Jack, I can't. I'm not so sure I don't need to just go home and wake up all over again. None of this can really be happening."

"I really *am* gonna go home if you don't come clean. You brought me here for a reason, so show me the goddamned exam room."

*****

When he'd heard about Kathryn's murder, Jack had expected blood. He had not envisioned the black liquid smeared on the walls, splattered on the floor and covering the autopsy table.

"So they're letting us conduct the investigation, but they took the video? That's not gonna make our job any easier," said Jack.

"You know what this black stuff is?" asked Olsen. "What in the human body can produce this crap?"

"You needed to ask Kathryn that question," said Jack, looking down at her covered body. It looked too small to be her.

"Yeah, well I didn't know I'd need an answer to that until she was already dead."

"Sorry."

"It's okay," said Olsen. He nodded toward the sheet on the floor. "Go ahead," he prompted.

Jack had seen dozens and dozens of dead bodies over the years. He did not often see those of people he knew.

A sound came from behind the men. A thump.

Jack, leaning to lift the sheet, looked back at Olsen. "What was that?"

"Remember when I told you Sims was showing signs of life?"

"Which is impossible because he was torn to pieces? Yeah."

Olsen turned to look at the drawer marked #2. He turned back to Jack, looked toward the bathroom and leapt over Kathryn's body in one jump, practically landing in the bathroom. Once inside, he dropped to his knees by the toilet and puked.

"Wayne, you okay, man?"

He shook his head but did not look up at Jack.

"Wayne. Why'd you keep everyone else out but us? This place should be swarming with forensics guys and detectives. What's with the perimeter?"

"Don't know. I just wanted you to see this. I've known you longer than practically anyone on the force, and I gotta be sure I'm not going crazy. Losing it, you know."

"So c'mon," said Jack, holding out his hand. Olsen took it and Jack pulled him up. The man was Jack's senior by twelve years, but Jack had been on the job when Wayne transferred in and worked his way up the ranks to Sheriff.

Before they left the bathroom, Wayne put a hand on Jack's shoulder and turned on the light. Black smears adorned the cover plate, too, but Wayne did not seem to be concerned with it.

Jack wasn't sure why; it was evidence, too. Everything in the entire vicinity was.

Once the door was closed, Olsen locked it. He looked into Jack's eyes. "This is the only place we don't have cameras. Jack, I gotta tell you what we're about to see."

"Or we could just see it."

Wayne shook his head for the hundredth time. "No. You can see it. I've seen enough."

"Man, you're really starting to worry me. What are you talking about?"

"When I got the call this morning I ordered the area sealed off. You know, big shot me, I wanted to be the first on scene. Nobody knew about Kathryn yet. Everyone believed the only crime was the murder of Ames."

"What about Kathryn? Didn't they notice her car in the lot?"

"She didn't park it in the lot. Came in at midday yesterday. Guess she figured on workin' late so there were no spaces open in the employee lot. She parked over on 2nd."

"I'm following you so far."

"When I got here I walked into this mess. Kathryn dead on the floor with a quarter of her gone. Just gone."

All the blood rushed from his face again and he dropped to his knees and threw up into the toilet for the second time.

Jack waited, then helped his friend back to his feet once more.

Wayne wiped his mouth with one sleeve. "When I got here, I came back here first. I saw Kathryn, but there was more."

"What?" asked Jack.

Wayne pointed. "There was more of this black shit – this ink, or whatever it is – on the face and handle of drawer #2. I'm a fucking detective at heart, so I went to the drawer and opened it."

"And?"

Wayne's face washed white again, but this time he didn't drop down to his knees. Instead, his desperate eyes stared into Jack's and he said, "Drawer two is where Justin Sims' body is. The kid is in pieces."

"All information I already knew, Wayne," said Jack. "I shot the scene pix, remember?"

"I opened that drawer, Jack. I saw the bag inside, moving around. I mean jumping."

"What the fuck was in it?" asked Jack, fascinated.

"All of Justin Sims is zipped inside that bag and locked inside that drawer, and all of him is alive."

"What?"

Wayne nodded toward it. "Check it yourself. Hold on."

Olsen left the room for a moment, then returned. "Okay, go," he said.

"What did you just go to do?"

"I turned off the video."

"Surveillance?"

Wayne nodded and looked at the drawer again. "Open it, Jack. You gotta prove to me that I'm not nuts."

Jack went to the drawer and grasped the handle. "You're saying he's alive in here."

Wayne nodded. "We didn't talk. Not sure he can."

Jack pulled the drawer open all the way. Sure enough, the shiny, black bag writhed and twisted on the rolling drawer shelf.

"What the fuck is in here, Olsen?" he asked. "Is this whole goddamned thing a joke?"

"You saw the dead girl in the street," said Olsen. "Open it, Jack!"

Jack reached for the zipper and moved away, holding it with two fingers. He took another half-step away and slid the zipper down slowly.

As he neared the end, horrified at what he was seeing, his eyes met those of Justin Sims. The young cop's head was still severed, but his eyes were open and even blinking.

He stared at Jack with something like recognition, then he began to scream. As he did so, black ooze bubbles popped from his lips before shattering. Somehow the thing coughed, spewing the black, almost odorless liquid against Jack's shirt. His freshly laundered shirt. He did not take notice at that moment.

A split-second later, it was as though he found his voice:

"Veselov!" Sims cried, his voice a powerful but gurgling sound, ten times more imposing than it had been in life. The very sound of it threatened to shatter the glass that encompassed them. "He killed me!"

Instinctively, Jack stood back and kicked the morgue door closed again, unwilling to touch it or anywhere near it with his bare hands. It slammed shut and he stared at Wayne. No words came to his mind, therefore none came from his lips. Wayne stared back, his face grim.

"This happened at 2:13 this morning," said Wayne.

"How do you know?"

"Because I watched the entire tape before I copied it onto a thumb drive and deleted it from the server."

"Thought you said the Feds took it."

"Wasn't sure I wanted to tell you the truth yet, man."

"Wayne, you could lose your job for that."

"I'm not sure I want the job anymore."

"Where did Sergei Veselov's body go?"

"It's not a body anymore, Jack."

"What the hell do you mean?"

Wayne pointed into the office. Across one wall where Jack remembered there was an enormous white board, hung a sheet. Wayne walked toward it and turned.

"He woke up, man." Wayne began to cry.

"Wayne, what the hell."

Olsen yanked the corner of the sheet and it fell away.

Smeared in blood, over eight feet wide and two feet long, was a single word: KROVOZHADNOST.

"What does it mean?" asked Jack.

"It's the name of Veselov's mafia. It translates roughly to bloodthirst."

"It's just intimidation," said Jack. "As for Sims, that's some kind of phenomenon you just haven't seen before. Nerve endings or something. All of this can be explained."

"I never took you for an idiot," said Wayne. "Go look at Kathryn's body. Now. That's an order."

Now it was Jack's turn to shake his head. He wasn't sure what was going on, but he also wasn't sure it wasn't some kind of elaborate, practical joke.

He shrugged, beginning to believe it all was a game. He actually laughed to himself. They must be bored, he thought.

Leaning down, he plucked the sheet from over the mound that was supposed to be Kathryn Hightower. He was certain she would pop up with a "Gotcha!" the moment he pulled it away.

He stared in horror. The vomit found its way into his throat before he could get to the bathroom. He leapt toward the wall of drawers and threw up against them, emptying his guts.

He looked up, realizing he was by the drawer where Sims' body was contained. As if on cue, from inside the drawer he heard Sims scream again, again gurgled but very clear: "Veselov! Bloodthirst!"

Jack staggered away from the wall of drawers, slipping in the black substance on the floor and falling backward. He landed with his head beside Kathryn's.

It was not attached to her body. He screamed and rolled away from it, scrambling to his knees, his eyes on the rest of her body. Her left arm was missing. The rest of her had bite marks and chunks gone.

Wayne stood in the doorway watching him.

"Where's her arm?"

"In here. I covered it with towels."

Both of Kathryn Hightower's breasts had been gouged off or removed in some other manner. The stomach appeared to have been chewed open and her rib cage was clearly visible, like the framework of a wooden, skeleton ship.

Jack, his heart pounding, scooted up to a sitting position, leaning back against the legs of the autopsy table. He looked over at Wayne, who stood staring at him.

"This ... none of this ... is possible," said Jack.

"But here we are."

"Where do we go from here, Wayne?" asked Jack. "Does the FBI really have anything?"

Wayne shook his head. "No. Nobody's been in here but us. I made sure of it."

"So you have the surveillance?"

"I do."

"Do I want to see it?"

Wayne shook his head. "Nobody wants to. But I'd appreciate it if you would."

"When and where?" asked Jack.

"We have to get Sims' body out of here."

"Where's Veselov?"

"Gone. Out there." Wayne's nod indicated the great, wide world. "Among the citizenry."

"Fuck."

"There were some samples Kathryn took before all this shit, I guess," said Wayne. "One's of this black stuff. The others are blood and urine samples."

"That's a start," said Jack. "Wayne, are you sure we shouldn't just bring someone in to figure this out?"

A thump came from Drawer #2. Both men jerked their heads toward it.

"We can't do anything to cover up Kathryn. We can claim the video didn't work. I'll just delete the digital files on it for a day or two. Fuckin' computer's so old and we still back it up with DAT tape."

"What's the reasoning here, Wayne."

"The public would freak out. Nobody would believe any of this, Jack. Big, murderous Russian comes to life and maybe eats our Medical Examiner. An entirely dismembered man comes back to life in a freezer drawer. Shit's the stuff of monster movies, man."

"I see your point," said Jack. "I don't see this ending well."

"Why should the end be any better than the beginning?" asked Wayne. "Let's get started. I'll go out and see what I can do about keeping our privacy."

"What are we going to do with Sims?"

"I'm thinkin' we take him to your place and question him."

"I don't have a fuckin' garage, Wayne, and he's not coming inside my house."

"Well, I've got a wife and kids," said Olsen. "You got a storage facility or something?"

"Can you spell surveillance cameras?" asked Jack.

"Okay, okay," said Wayne. "My garage, then. I can keep my wife out. I'll tell her we're working on my bikes or something."

"Go do your thing then. I'll try to get Sims zipped back inside the bag."

"Gag him."

"What?"

"If he screams when we're taking him out of here we're fucked."

Jack shook his head. "Maybe I need to go home and wake up again. Because I can't be awake yet."

"It's something to hold onto," said Wayne. "Hurry.

*****

Wayne had gone to get his bag containing the thumb drive with the surveillance footage on it, along with a large duffel in which to stuff Officer Sims. A body bag was immediately recognizable as such, and there was no way Jack was going to sling one of them over his shoulder and walk out of there.

Jack stood and stared at drawer #2. He rested his open palm against it and held it there. Nothing.

He breathed in and out, closing his eyes. Without opening them, he turned to where Kathryn's body lay and inhaled deeply once more.

Jack opened his eyes.

Kathryn was still there. His left hand was still on drawer #2, and he felt a thump.

"Goddamnit!" he shouted. It was as real as it had been a few moments ago, which meant that all of this shit was way, way out of his league.

He steeled his nerves and pulled open the drawer. He slammed it again.

Gloves. He needed fucking gloves. Double gloves. He went to the dispenser labeled L on the wall and plucked four gloves from it, snapping them onto his hands.

He opened the drawers until he found some gauze. The black stuff was smeared here, too. Veselov? Why would he have been in the drawer?

No matter. It could not have been Veselov. Veselov was dead as dead could be. "There's a logical

93

explanation for all of this," he said aloud, his voice like tin to his ears, hollow and weak.

"Okay," he said, pulling the drawer open.

He slid it all the way out and pulled the zipper down farther, opening the top. Sims stared at him, his eyes wide and frantic.

"Got to find the Russian," he gurgled. "Want ... hungry." His teeth snapped and Jack reached in, grabbed the severed head and turned it away from him.

With shaking hands, Jack unwrapped the roll of 4" wide gauze and reached back inside the bag. He clutched a handful of Sims' hair and lifted the head out of the bag. It was as heavy as a bowling ball. Jack hadn't expected it.

The barf charged up from his stomach, and without letting go of the head, he ran around the autopsy table, jumped over Kathryn's upper body and staggered into the bathroom. As he passed the sink he dropped Sims' head in the sink and slammed the door behind him, falling to his knees where Wayne had expelled his breakfast just minutes before.

"Bloodthirst!" called Sims from the sink, and the vomit felt good rushing from his body. Jack wished it would continue, because he did not want to face the task at hand.

Please, please, he thought. Let me pass out or something. Someone else can deal with this.

"Veselov!" shouted Sims.

The bubbling sound of Sims' voice was worse than his puke blending with Olsen's in the toilet. He had to shut him up. Jack reached up and flushed the toilet, and scrambled to his feet. He rushed to the sink, and when

Sims' head was in the middle of another shouted, *Bloodthirst!*, Jack started the gauze.

Glad for the gloves, he tried to avoid Sims' staring eyes as he brought the roll around and around, placing the head on its stump of a neck on the corner of the sink. When he had effectively covered the mouth, he kept wrapping it over the thing's eyes until the gauze ran out.

The screams were now muffles. The eyes could no longer stare at him.

Jack opened the door and saw the room still empty. He went over and placed the head back in the body bag, alongside all the other writhing body parts. He turned to see Wayne standing three feet behind him.

"How's your thing going?"

Jack staggered back, almost falling, but caught himself on another drawer handle, his heart slamming.

"Jesus!" shouted Jack. "Jesus Christ, Wayne!"

"Sorry, sorry, man," said Wayne. "I got the bag. I didn't mean to scare you."

"Well, then you just say something when you come in the room, man! Let's call that a rule right now, from now on. Just say some fucking words when you walk into a room where I'm handling moving dead parts!"

"Are we fuckin' crazy, Jack?" asked Wayne. There was a slight smile on his lips. "I was in the other room there and I just started laughing like a crazy person. I really think this crap might be making me insane."

"I don't know. About Kathryn. You going to leave Kathryn's other arm in there?"

Jack walked into the room where the scrawled message was and moved the towels. Her arm lay on the floor, palm up.

"She's not going to start moving when I pick it up, right?"

"I have no idea. After I found Sims in the drawer I watched her a while. Never saw a twitch."

"Okay," said Jack, his mind running a mile a second. He knelt down and reached for it, stopping midstream. He looked at Wayne. "Maybe it takes longer than we know."

"Leave it," said Wayne. "This is a crime scene, so we won't screw with things too much. Hopefully, they'll just figure someone busted in, killed Ames and Kathryn and stole Veselov's and Sims' bodies. I'll try to lead it in that direction if anyone asks my opinion."

"And they'll figure the reason for the killing and the body thefts was ... what?"

Wayne shrugged. "Russian mafia shit. Hell, I don't know." He walked back into the other room and Jack followed, his head swimming with impossibilities.

"Let's transfer the body bag into this one," said Wayne. "I think it'll do."

Together they lifted the bag out and rested it on the floor. Wayne opened the duffel and unzipped it all the way.

"Sure nobody's going to come in here?" asked Jack.

"At the risk of being fired or demoted, no."

In ten minutes of stuffing and tucking, they got Sims inside. He fought it all the way.

"Which way?"

"Out the front," said Wayne. "You got him gagged?"

"A task I'll not soon forget."

"Sorry about that."

Jack shook his head. "Once you tell them about Kathryn, you know they're gonna page me to shoot this scene. And Ames, too. You'll have to go and wait for me."

"Shit," said Olsen. "I'm an idiot. Why didn't I think of that?"

"I don't know," said Jack. "Other stuff on your mind?"

This time both men laughed. It wasn't uncomfortable. It was a release. Shared insanity.

They figured out their next moves.

As Jack did his best to look minimally burdened, he hauled the very heavy duffel out the front door, beneath the crime scene tape and out to Wayne's truck. Meanwhile, Sheriff Olsen let the world know that the Russian's body had been stolen, Sims' body had been stolen, and Medical Examiner Kathryn Hightower and security guard Paul Ames had been killed.

There would be many questions.

Jack hoped Sims could provide some answers.

He was terrified at the thought of what the living dead cop had become.

*****

Sergei had searched the other cabinets in the Medical Examiner's building and had found bagged clothing. Nothing was large enough, but he did find a 2XL tee shirt and some jeans that would not button. He used a belt on its last punched hole to hold them up. There were no shoes in a fourteen, so he was barefoot as he ran out into the night.

The guard had been searching his desk for something when Sergei had emerged from the hallway. As his surprised face jerked upward, Sergei was there as fast as a cat, slamming his head down into the desktop and snapping his neck.

The power within him was intense and exhilarating.

Later on, he stood in the shadows a few blocks to the southwest. The small, blue house with pink shutters on the corner of Aldridge and Beacon Streets looked deserted. Sergei walked casually along the sidewalk, the clothes barely covering his 6'5" frame, giving him the perfectly acceptable appearance of a homeless man.

The invisible occupiers of the cities; people did not so much stare at them as avoid looking at all costs, afraid they would be hit up for a buck or two.

That worked for Sergei's purpose.

He went up to the house and stood on the doorstep, listening. The streetlight directly in front of the home was out. Normally it was a drug dealer's trick, but it may have just been burned out.

After five minutes hearing no sounds, he knocked and eased open the torn screen door. It squealed.

No lights came on inside. More confident, Sergei knocked again.

No dogs barking. No feet padding toward the door.

He tried the knob; locked.

He inspected the windows for alarm company stickers and found none. Glancing behind him quickly, Veselov shouldered the door hard and with a crack of the frame, it pushed inward and he slipped inside.

Once in, he pushed the door closed again and hammered the splintered wood back into position with the palm of his hand to keep it closed. Then he turned the deadbolt, which had not previously been engaged.

The hum of the air conditioner told him the power was on. He allowed his eyes to adjust to the darkness more before moving down a narrow hall just beyond the entry. When he reached the kitchen, he turned on the light.

He went in and stood in front of the sink, taking in the floor plan. As he faced the rear of the house, which was the direction he felt himself pulled, off to his right was a door. It was closed.

He turned and saw a small family room to his left with another door, probably leading to a hall and perhaps a bathroom.

He did not have to shit or piss. He pondered his condition again and wondered if he ever would.

Veselov turned left and entered the family room, then walked into the hallway. As suspected, a bathroom was just to the right as he entered. Just across on the left was an open door. He poked his head in and hit the light switch. It had pictures of beaches and palm trees, faded yellow with age. He looked down. The carpet was green shag. The bedding featured a quilted spread.

The room smelled of mothballs.

He turned off the light and left the room. Nothing else back there but a linen closet. He opened the door and removed a threadbare towel. If he had to fire the gun he had taken from the guard, it would suppress the noise if wrapped around the barrel. Not that he wanted to fire it if it wasn't absolutely necessary. He only had one extra magazine, so conservation would be necessary until he had accomplished all that he must.

Whatever it was. It still wasn't clear to Sergei.

As far as pursuers, they would be looking for the person who wreaked havoc on the Medical Examiner. They would not be looking for a living Sergei Veselov, he knew. He had left Sims there for the very reason that such a phenomenon might distract them from finding him.

As he walked back down the hall toward the kitchen, he stopped. A tingling from his back. Veselov turned and stared into the darkness.

He wanted to walk toward it and not stop until he reached whatever destination called to him; the pull was powerful and persistent. After an indeterminate amount of time, he turned and continued toward the other side of the old house.

The closed door lay ahead. Sergei began to tingle as he drew closer to it.

*****

The Russian turned the knob and pushed the door inward. He heard a ceiling fan humming. The air conditioner had cut off for the moment.

Now he heard soft snores. He removed his .45 from his pants and held it in his right hand, a round already chambered. He wrapped the towel in his hands around the barrel to quiet its report should he find it necessary to fire the weapon.

His eyes had adjusted to the light of that room, and with the soft glow of moonlight through the draperies, he could see a single mound in the middle of the bed.

He found he was starving. Ravenous, in fact. As he had been just over an hour ago when he had consumed much of the woman whose name tag read K. Hightower, Medical Examiner.

"I hear you, and there is a gun pointed at your chest," came the voice of an old man.

As Sergei watched, the covers fell and a man's hand was revealed. It was too dark to tell what type, but in that hand was a pistol of some kind.

"I am only hungry," said Sergei, playing on the homeless theme. "I want only to eat something." It wasn't a lie; but for what did he hunger?

"You coulda eaten out there, but you're in here. That means you want more than food. Now get out of here right now or I'll kill you."

Sergei raised his gun and was met by a *thwump!*

He felt something hit him around his left ribcage, and reached up to feel. Something wet coated his fingers. He pressed in where he had felt the pressure and a rib moved. The bullet had broken a rib. There was no pain.

Veselov moved his hand around to his back and felt what was probably the exit wound, leaking out the same wetness.

"You fired before giving me a chance to leave," said Veselov. "You are not a man of your word."

Now the man pulled the chain on the light beside him and the room illuminated. The gun in his hand was a suppressed semi-automatic of some kind.

"Why do you have a silencer?" asked Veselov. "It seems to me that you would want your neighbors to hear you fire so they could call the police."

101

"I shot you!" shouted the thin, gray-haired man, his hands both gripping the gun, trembling. "What is that black shit all over you?"

Veselov looked down at the wound and saw the black liquid running down his borrowed shirt and pants.

He looked up and the man fired again, this time striking Sergei in the left thigh. Veselov rushed toward him, grabbed his wrist and snapped it in two. With a twist, he ripped the old man's hand from his body and the gun fell away.

The man had time to utter only a light whimper before Veselov used the old man's own severed hand to beat him into unconsciousness.

As the old man's warm, red blood leaked onto the floor, Veselov unwrapped the thin towel from his gun and used it to tie a makeshift tourniquet around the man's bloody wrist stump.

Sergei plucked the wallet from the nightstand and opened it.

Larry Peale. Born March 22, 1939. He removed the money from the wallet, not sure if he would need it or not.

Larry was still alive. Sergei sat on the side of his bed and lifted the hand to his lips, allowing the still dripping blood to touch his dried tongue.

A sudden hunger overtook him.

He tore at the flesh with his teeth, staring at the old man's rising and falling chest on the bed beside him.

As he felt the warm blood running down his throat, he realized that the longer Peale remained alive, the more strength he would gain from him.

I am eating his life force. From his pumping heart to my body. It will make me unstoppable.

Sergei Veselov again turned to stare toward the sliding glass door. The west lay beyond. As he consumed the hand, he felt his strength grow.

By the morning he would be powerful. He would head west then.

*****

CHAPTER FOUR

Jack Hunger drove his own car behind Sheriff Olsen's Dodge truck, his mind hammering at the problem they faced. He did not know how the condition of Kathryn Hightower's body would be explained, but Olsen would likely do what it took to keep the details out of the press.

Olsen pulled into the driveway of his home just off McGregor Parkway in Fort Myers, and Jack parked in front of the house. If Wayne got an emergency call, they may not be in a position to leave, what with Sims' condition. He hoped Wayne had duct tape. It was the only gag that Jack trusted.

"Help me with this thing, would you?" asked Jack, opening the tailgate of the truck.

"Leave it for now and come inside," said Wayne, holding his briefcase in his hand. "Surveillance."

Jack stared at him. He almost responded that he did not want to see the footage, but he had to. This was too impossible not to analyze from start to finish, and if they actually could finish it, then it was better for the world that they do.

He nodded and followed Wayne into the house.

*****

After watching the computer screen for almost an hour, Jack said, "Wow."

"I get sick just thinkin' about it," said Wayne.

"So it was 2:12 in the morning. That was the moment Veselov opened his eyes."

Wayne looked at Jack. "Think Sims woke up at the same time?"

"We can ask him," said Jack.

"So far all he does is scream about Veselov."

"He's a little upset, which I can understand."

"Jack, we can't tell anyone about any of this. This is crazy shit, and I'm not willing to share it with Lee County or the world. I say whatever this is, we gotta stop it."

Jack wasn't sure it was stoppable. "Are you thinking this is the first time this has ever happened?"

"I have no idea," said Wayne. "You ever heard of it?"

"In the movie Reanimator, yeah," said Jack. "Pretty much just like this."

"Whatever. This can't get out. If I have to take a leave of absence for a few days, I will. You need to do what you gotta do, too. Until it's done."

Jacked stared at Wayne for a moment and said, "Wayne. That dead man – that completely dead man – woke up. He killed Kathryn Hightower and he systematically devoured her. Outside is another like him. I wonder what his tastes are."

"He's a cop," said Olsen. "Not a murderer."

"I somehow doubt that Sergei Veselov, Russian Mafia or not, ever ate his enemies. This coming back to life shit might just change you a little."

"Acknowledged. We're still on our own," said Wayne.

Jack sighed. "So we get Sims and get started?"

"Let me just tell Barbara we're gonna do some stuff in the garage. Like I said, I'll just tell her it's bike related and she'll want nothing to do with it."

"After the news?" asked Jack. "She had to have seen the news by now."

Wayne smiled and shook his head. "Nope. Believe it or not, she doesn't watch that shit. She spends the day home schooling Corrine and Jillian and after that she watches Dr. Phil and crap like that."

"Your girls are here?" Jack knew they were eleven and thirteen years old, and could be nosy and playful with their dad. "Can you keep them out of the garage? Wayne, this is too fuckin' scary to take the chance. I guess I just assumed ... I don't know. They'd be at school."

"Pulled 'em out of school last year. Got too weird with me being sheriff. Threats and shit."

"You never told me that."

Wayne shrugged. "I was never that worried. It was Barb."

"When you get inside open the garage door, would you?"

"Yeah," said Wayne. "Shoulda done it from the truck. Just a minute."

In thirty seconds the garage door rolled up and Jack hoisted the bag from the back of Olsen's truck and hauled it into the garage. He rested it on a waist-high work bench and left it zipped for the moment.

Five minutes later, Wayne came out and hit the door close button. It rolled down smoothly and he turned on the light.

"This is real, right?" asked Wayne, his face grim.

"It was last time I had this bag open."

The bag suddenly twitched, like something inside had kicked.

"Still is," said Wayne. "I need a fucking Xanax."

"Or three," said Jack.

"Latex gloves are in the drawer right in front of you. Hold on a sec before you get him out."

"Never said I was gonna do it," said Jack, opening the drawer and removing two pairs of latex gloves. He snapped a pair on and tossed the others to Wayne, who had just returned from propping a small stepladder with rubber feet beneath the doorknob. Now the door could not open into the garage. Wayne walked to the garage door opener and pulled the rope hanging down from the motor, disengaging the gear.

"Nobody's getting in here now," he said. "Just another minute."

He went to a drawer in his tool chest, used his keys to unlock it, and slid the drawer open. From it, he removed a bottle of Jack Daniel's.

He unscrewed the cap as he walked toward Jack, his eyes never leaving his friend's until he took a deep pull

107

ERIC A. SHELMAN

from the Tennessee whiskey. "Here," he said, handing it over.

Jack took it and looked at it. "Wayne, it's not even noon."

"I don't have any pot. If you want to numb yourself a little bit before we open this bag, now's your opportunity."

"What if you get called?"

"It's bound to happen," said Wayne. "I'll stall. Veselov's out there, so we have to put on our fuckin' big boy pants and dive in."

Jack turned the bottle to his lips and took two large swallows. It might have been smooth, but it was lost on Jack. Beer was smooth. This was like lighter fluid.

He gave the bottle back to Wayne, who capped it and placed it on the counter. "Unzip it."

Jack held one end of the bag and slid the zipper across. The smell, which had been somewhat all encompassing in the morgue, blasted him in the face.

"Jesus!" said Wayne. "He may be alive, but he sure smells deader'n shit."

"Think he's still rotting, even though he's kind of alive?" asked Jack.

"Well, your theory's acceptable since none of this is possible anyway," said Wayne. "Let's take his head out first."

"Be my guest," said Jack, stepping aside.

Wayne rubbed his thinning hair and glared at Jack. He reached in and tried to situate Sims' head, Jack assumed so he could lift it without touching his face. Jack wasn't sure whether it was out of respect for Sims or to avoid the heebie jeebies factor of palming a living dead man's face.

He lifted the head out. The gauze had pulled into his mouth somewhat, and his teeth gnawed at it while his tongue jutted out as though trying to push the material aside. All of it was to no avail. Once Olsen had the head clear of the bag, he said, "Why'd you blindfold him?"

"He was staring at me."

Wayne shrugged. "Guess we should've figured out where to put it," said Jack, scanning the garage. He spotted a small, Igloo Playmate cooler. "Hold on."

"Hurry, buddy," said Wayne."

He retrieved the cooler, cleared a place out on the shelf above the workbench, and turned the cooler on its side. He said, "Just tuck it right in there, facing out."

"No shit," said Wayne.

He slid the head in the cooler, and pulled the Ace bandage from over Sims' eyes. They darted back and forth, obviously curious, but he did not look as panicked as when they had first seen him. He was clearly listening to everything they said, and they were not yet discussing how to get rid of him or how to put him back to dead.

The head kept tilting forward. "Shit," said Wayne. "I can't … it's not staying."

"You got duct tape?" Jack asked.

"Yeah, toolbox against the wall behind us, top drawer."

Jack got the duct tape and tore off a length. He taped it across the opening of the ice chest, and Wayne eased Sims' head forward until it rested against the sticky part of the tape.

"There."

"Perfect. Now let's cut that gauze," said Jack.

"I might have to puke first," said Wayne.

"I know," Jack said. "The smell."

"The fuckin' thought's enough."

"Scissors?" Jack asked.

"Jar on top of the toolbox," said Wayne.

Jack retrieved them and carried them over. Holding the scissors where Sims could see them, he looked into Sims' eyes and spoke in as soothing a tone as he could muster through his terror at the situation: "Justin, I know you're confused. So are we. We need to take this gag off your mouth and ask you some questions. You can't scream or yell or anything because Wayne's family is in the house a few feet away. Now move your eyes up and down if we're on the same page so far."

Jack got dizzy when Officer Justin Sims' obeyed his instructions. His eyes went up and down. The mere thought of talking to a severed head made Jack want to pass out.

He tried to shrug it off. It took almost a full thirty seconds.

"Jack?" asked Wayne. "You okay?"

Jack shook his head no and went on: "So here's the deal. You know me and you absolutely know Sheriff Olsen. We don't know how you got this way or how Veselov came back to life. Whatever caused it is probably the same thing that happened to you, so we're going to take that gag off and we're going to have a rational question and answer period."

Rational, thought Jack. *That'll be the day.*

"Cut away," said Wayne.

Jack reached up and pulled the gauze away from Sims' mouth. His mouth opened and he tried to catch his finger with his teeth, but Jack jerked it away.

"What the fuck!" he said, glaring at him.

Sims' eyes looked confused, and he furrowed his brow.

"Cut over by his cheek," said Wayne. "Stay away from his mouth. Now we need to know what the fuck that's about."

Jack gave Wayne the scissors. "You, man. Now I'm shaking too bad."

Wayne followed his own instructions and peeled away the gauze. Once it was clear, Sims would not shut up.

"Veselov," he said. "Bloodthirst. Krovozhadnost! I must ... find Veselov! Kill Veselov!"

"Veselov's already dead, Deputy Sims," said Wayne. "So are you, for that matter."

"Dead. Not dead. Find Veselov."

"Sims, we need you to focus and listen. Can you do that?" asked Wayne.

"Yeah," the voice bubbled. As the thing spoke, black coated its teeth and black veins jagged across the whites of the eyes like dark lightning strikes. Like bloodshot, but black.

"Why do you want to find Veselov?" asked Jack.

"First ... tell me. What happened."

Wayne took a deep breath and looked at Jack. He looked back at Sims.

"I know this is a strange question," said Wayne, "but how do you feel right now."

111

"I feel like I'm wrapped in plastic wrap," he said. "My whole body."

"Like you're swaddled? Like a baby?"

"I wouldn't have put it like that, but yeah. Sheriff Olsen, what's going on?"

Wayne reached over and dragged the duffel toward him.

"What are you doing?" asked Jack.

"I'm gonna show him the rest of him."

Jack took the bottle of whiskey from the bench, unscrewed the cap and took a long drink. He gave it to Wayne who followed suit.

"Good idea," said Wayne.

"I'll get one end. You get the other."

Jack lifted the end, and Wayne got the other. Sims' eyes darted back and forth. "What's in the bag?" he asked.

"You were in there a minute ago with them," said Jack.

"It was dark. I thought I saw a hand."

"Ready?" asked Jack.

"No."

"Now."

They tilted the bag forward and Sims' head gasped, his eyes wide. "Is ... is that ... how is this possible?"

"It's you. And we don't know." Wayne shrugged.

"It's not me," said Sims.

"I'm gonna do this once," said Jack. He reached inside the bag and lifted out one of the severed arms. It was bare. The uniform had been bagged separately.

"No distinguishing marks on .... Let's see ... it's the right arm."

112

"I don't have any tattoos," said Sims.

"Okay, give me a thumbs up with your right hand," said Wayne.

Jack gripped the arm. "This thing's heavier than I expected."

The four fingers curled in and the thumb stuck straight out. Jack then turned the arm, positioning it correctly.

Sims stared at his arm in Jack's hands, his expression one of horror. He gave a bubbling sigh and passed out.

"Did he just ... pass out?" asked Jack.

"He did."

"So this is a shock to him too?" asked Jack.

"Apparently so. Maybe he needs a pull off this JD."

Jack leaned forward and lightly shook the cooler. The head bobbled back and forth and the eyes flitted open.

"Whoa," said Sims.

"You get it now?" Wayne said. "Look Sims, I'm sorry, but Veselov tore you apart. *You died.* SWAT killed the shit out of him less than an hour later. Last night ... technically, early this morning, you both woke up." He turned to stare at Jack. "Right? I mean ... *he's* awake, and he says he saw Veselov alive, so what are we dealing with here ... reanimation shit, right? Fuckin' hell."

Jack shrugged and shook his head. "If I think about it too much ... I don't know. This is a really, really tough one."

Sims' had apparently tuned out after Wayne's comments; his mouth dropped open and black inkiness ran out. "My God," he gurgled.

Jack's eyes searched the counter until he found a small Gerber jar that once held creamed corn but that now held washers. He dumped the contents onto the counter and pushed the jar beneath the dripping, black stream.

"You okay, Sims?" asked Wayne.

Sims wrinkled his face. "Excuse me, Sheriff, but that was a fucking stupid question."

"I knew it the second it left my pie hole."

Sims looked at Jack. "Can you put me together?" he asked.

"What?" asked Wayne. "For what?"

"I need to find Veselov," he said. "Find him ... and kill ... him."

"You want to kill him?" asked Wayne, looking at Jack.

"I will kill him!"

"Stop yelling or we put the gag back on, Sims, and that's an order! We need to know how this happened and how to stop it." Wayne looked nervously at the door to the house.

Sims closed his eyes for probably fifteen seconds. When he opened them, he appeared to have calmed somewhat. Amazingly, his head nodded on its stub of a neck. "I'll stop." His eyes did not leave Jack.

"Good," said Wayne. "Okay, Deputy Sims. How are you going to find him? You keep saying you'll kill him, well, that's the first job. You gotta know where he is."

"That's just it!" said Sims. "I have a feeling – like a really strong force pulling me to him. It's all I can think about, but I can't do anything when I'm like this."

"Humor him, Wayne," said Jack.

"Fine," said Wayne. "Okay. If we were to be able to put you back on a body and you became mobile – and I'm telling you this is never going to happen – where would you go?"

"That way," gurgled the voice, turning his eyes to the southwest. As the head spoke, black juice of some kind ran from its mouth, down its chin and dripped from the cooler.

"That stuff never seems to run out," said Jack. He adjusted the baby food jar that was now half-full.

"Why would you go that way?" asked Wayne.

"Veselov *is* there."

"He's there. For sure." Wayne stared at him.

"Yes."

"How do you know?" asked Jack, staring at the severed head in the cooler.

"I'm drawn … there. Pulled. I need to GO! WANT TO KILL HIM!"

"Shut the fuck up!" shouted Wayne, yanking the cooler down from the shelf, turning it upright and pivoting the lid closed and latched.

Jack stared at him. A knock came on the garage door and the knob turned. Now the ladder propped beneath the knob rocked as someone tried to open the door.

"Honey?" asked Barbara from the other side. "Are you okay? What was that yelling? Why is this door barred?"

"Go on back to your schooling, honey," said Wayne. "We're using a pretty smelly solvent on the Harley right now and I didn't want you guys walking in here and choking."

"You wearing a mask?" she asked.

"Putting them on now," said Wayne, realizing his voice was not muffled so she would recognize the lie if he had told it.

"Be careful in there," she said. "and open the side door to vent."

"Yes, dear," said Wayne, eyeing Jack, then the closed cooler.

After she'd gone, Jack slid the lid open on the Playmate again and looked inside. Sims' face stared upward. "We must ... go after Veselov," Sims said.

Jack lifted the cooler back up onto the shelf, placed it on its end again, and situated the dead officer's head. "Sorry about that, but this is kind of delicate as I'm sure you grasp. Your yelling got the Sheriff's wife in here."

"If you can't answer any questions, then you're not doing us any good," said Wayne. "You say you can take us to the Russian?"

"I can ... guide you. I ... have to ... kill him."

"Why do you feel you have to do that?" Jack asked.

"I ... don't know. It's ... fuck I'm hungry."

Jack looked at Wayne, then back at Sims' head. "You don't know?"

"Are my feet moving in that bag?" asked Sims. "Tell me, please."

The bag was jumping on the bench just out of Sims' view. "Yeah, it looks like a sack full of Mexican jumping beans," said Wayne.

116

"Wayne," said Jack. "We might be able to do what he wants."

Wayne stared at him.

Jack looked at a rack suspended from the ceiling. He pointed. "That's rebar up there. You've got duct tape. I assume you have some jeans and a shirt and stuff. Preferably long sleeved."

"Do you fucking hear yourself?" asked Wayne.

"Officer Sims, do you feel any pain at all?"

"No," he said.

Jack reached into the duffel bag and withdrew Sims' left arm. He hoisted it onto the work bench and took a paint stir stick off a shelf on the wall. Next, he snapped the stick in two so it had a sharp point. "I'm going to poke this into your … well, the meaty part. Tell me if you feel it."

"Jeez, Jack," said Wayne.

"We have to know." He pushed it in gently, watching Sims' face.

"Are you doing it yet? I can't see," said Sims.

Jack pushed it in an inch. "Yeah. It's in a ways."

"No," said Sims. "Nothing."

Jack nodded, withdrew the stick and put it aside, leaving the arm on the counter. "Okay, so we know he can't feel pain, Wayne. We can make him look somewhat normal," said Jack. "He wants to find Veselov and we need to find him. He's about as dangerous as they come. He was a killer before, but he might be ten times as dangerous now, based on what he did to Kathryn."

"What did he do?" asked Sims.

"He … he killed her and he …" Wayne stopped mid-sentence.

"He … ate her?" asked Sims.

Jack and Wayne jerked their heads toward Sims.

"I was guessing," he said.

"Uh, good guess," said Jack.

Wayne grabbed the bottle of whiskey and drank a deep swallow. "I'm talking to a severed head in a cooler," he said.

"I'm in a cooler?" asked Sims.

"You wanna see?" asked Wayne.

"We need a mirror," said Jack. "I don't think he really gets it."

"I don't have a mirror out here," said Wayne. "But hold on."

He pulled out his cell phone and put it in camera mode. He then flipped it to video and started filming. He turned the camera on Sims' head for a few moments, then pulled open the duffel bag.

"Wiggle your fingers and toes," he said.

The bag started vibrating, and Wayne filmed inside. After a few seconds, he stopped filming and turned the screen toward Sims.

"This is what you are now, Deputy," said Wayne. "I'm sorry."

As they watched Sims watch the video, black, inky tears rolled from his eyes, and his black mouth hung open, the tongue the same dark color.

"No," he said, his voice thick.

"Like I said, sorry," said Wayne. "But we need your help to find Veselov. We'll kill him for you, but we need to stop him."

"Hungry," said Sims.

"You saw ... you don't have any ... any body," said Jack.

"I understand," said Sims.

Jack slammed his hands down on the work bench. "You understand? Seriously ? I wish the hell I did. Do you know how this happened? What did you feel? When did it happen?"

"I was in the house, on the porch. I got knocked out and when I woke up I was in terrible pain and I saw that big fucker holding my arm and using it as a marker on the wall."

"Die tin man," said Olsen.

"What?" said Sims.

"That's what he wrote on the wall."

"I musta been out," said Sims.

Wayne shrugged. "Ya think? What's the next thing you remember?"

"Then I was in the dark," said Sims. "It was cold and stuffy, and things kept moving and shifting around against me. Pitch black."

"Well, that was obviously you shifting against you, and because you were in a refrigerator it was cold, and because you were in a body bag, it was dark.

"How did you know about Veselov?" asked Jack.

"He opened the drawer and unzipped the bag, I guess. I saw a gash of light and his face appeared above me. I fucking recognized him. The bastard laughed, then I heard the zipper and it was dark again."

"Is that how you know about Veselov?" asked Jack.

"I might have been unconscious on the porch, but he woke me up before he started tearing me apart."

"Nice of him," said Wayne.

"When I saw him from inside that bag, I wanted to kill him instantly, like instinct," said Sims. "I want to kill him now. *Help me.*"

"What was your idea again? Put him back together like fucking Humpty Dumpty?" asked Wayne.

"What the hell else we gonna do?" asked Jack. "Mount his head on the dashboard and use him like a fuckin' GPS?"

"Maybe. I don't know," said Wayne. "We need to get rid of the rest of him. Maybe burn it."

"I'm *right* here!" said Sims, his eyes darting side-to-side. "Let him tell you his idea!"

Wayne sighed. "What's your idea, princess?"

"I can walk the hell out of here and let you deal with this on your own, Olsen."

"Sheriff Olsen to you," he said. He winked. "Sorry."

"Okay, Just listen," said Jack. "We get that rebar and we cut it into the right lengths. I see you've got a bench mount brush and grinder wheel there. We grind the rebar to points, and we basically jam it into the pieces of his arms, leg and torso like dowels and then we duct tape him together."

"Did you work this out some other day, or just now?" asked Wayne.

"That's a good idea," said Sims. "Are my knees okay?"

"The fucking price goes up if you keep chipping in," said Wayne. "Relax, Sims."

"He's right. If the knees are broken they won't hold him. We'll have to make a joint or something."

Wayne stared. "Jack, this isn't an erector set, buddy. This is a dead guy who's not dead!"

"We give the guy some mobility and he helps us find the crazy Russian."

"Come outside with me for a second, would you?" asked Wayne.

Jack rolled his eyes and followed Wayne. He unlocked the side door and opened it, stepping out into the sun. "What do we do with him afterward?"

"I didn't think of that."

"We have no idea how to kill the parts."

"No," said Jack. "We don't."

"So ... what?"

"We figure it out. Cross that bridge when we come to it. You know. Police work. Think on our feet."

"Fair enough," said Wayne. "Let's figure out how many pieces of rebar we're going to need. And you're doing the head."

*****

"I really need to have a nap," said Jack.

"I'm retiring after this," said Wayne.

"Wayne, you're like fifty-two."

"Fuck it. With this crap, I've had enough."

Each man had emptied his stomach a minimum of three times during the process of inserting the rebar dowels when reassembling his body. The mere handling of twitching, jerking body parts was unsettling, but Jack's stomach turned at the raw, human meat. So, apparently, did Wayne's.

121

ERIC A. SHELMAN

The arm dowels were different from the ones fashioned for the legs, and a bit shorter; they had to bend them into an L shape. The small end of the L pushed into the shoulder socket, and the longer end into the meat of the arms. They used several lengths of baling wire to distribute the weight of the extremities over a wider area of solid flesh. Once they wrapped the duct tape around the arm connection points, they wrapped it several times around the chest and returned to wrap the arms yet again.

In the end, they hung and moved very well.

Jack hadn't been convinced it would work. The arms were much heavier than he expected, and the severed leg was so heavy they had to use not only baling wire, but rebar-fashioned external fixators on each side. Once in place, they wrapped the hell out of them with duct tape.

Jack was now worried about the right leg. Veselov had broken it at the knee, but had clearly run out of steam before he could tear it off.

Sims' headless body lay in the middle of the garage, as they held the remaining roll of duct tape and looked at his floppy right leg.

"Move it again," said Wayne, looking at Sims' head in the Playmate.

Sims moved his right leg. It flopped and he had no control.

"I think it's pretty clear it's still not going to support him," said Wayne.

"Let's figure out his head now and we'll fine-tune his body after we get him looking kind of whole."

"Be my guest," said Wayne.

"Sims, do I need to worry about damaging your brain?" asked Jack.

Sims gave him a sarcastic look. "How would I know? I recommend being careful."

"What, like a zombie?" asked Wayne. "You think if you poke into his brain you'll kill him?"

Jack stared at Wayne. "Outside."

Wayne shrugged and walked toward the door. Jack followed and stepped onto the concrete pad, pulling the door closed behind them.

"That's not a bad idea," said Jack. "As B movie as it sounds, when we're done with him it might be worthwhile."

"Fucker already died once. Now he's gotta die again."

Jack shrugged. "There's nowhere for him. He's our responsibility."

They both agreed to try brain trauma later, but for now they would just be careful. They went back inside.

"What's the verdict?" asked Sims.

"Let's get your head out of the cooler," said Jack.

"We're going to need a single pin straight down into the neck," said Wayne. "So he can pivot his head."

"Yeah, but to avoid poking directly into his brain, there should be two uprights that can go on either side, like a goalpost," said Jack. "Maybe go on either side of his brain."

"I'm pretty sure the brain fills his head cavity, Doctor Hunger."

"You know what?" said Jack.

"What?"

"What?" said Sims.

123

"We can't spend all day fabricating a skeleton for Sims here." He nodded to Wayne and took three steps across the garage. Wayne followed again.

"What?" Wayne whispered.

"Screw this, man. We jam the rebar straight up there as far as we can. He was dead before so if he dies again, good. One less insane situation we need to deal with. We'll be able to track a walking dead man mountain like Veselov pretty easily anyway, right?"

"You sure?"

"Yeah."

"Forsaking all things George Romero?"

"That's fiction. This isn't."

"What are you guys talking about?" asked Sims, behind them. They both turned.

"Nothin' Sims," said Wayne. "Head reattachment engineering talk."

"I might have some ideas," Sims said.

"We got it worked out. Ready?"

"Excuse me if I don't nod," said Sims.

Jack put on new gloves, then put another pair on over them. He lifted Sims' head from the cooler and lay it on a folded towel on the work bench.

"Ready, Sims?"

The head was resting on its right cheek. Sims said, "Yeah."

Holding the rebar in his right hand, Jack used his left hand to press the head down firmly. He positioned the rebar in the center of the opening and pushed it in about an inch. The sound of compressing meat tickled his gag reflex, but he fought the feeling.

"You alright?" he asked.

124

"So far," said Sims.

"Not so sure about me," said Wayne. "Just like cold water. Just dive in, Jackie."

Jack turned his head and plunged the rebar in until he felt the end hit the top of the skull. The moment he hit bottom, he released it and paced away, across the garage.

"Wow," he said. "I'm not cut out for this kind of work."

Wayne picked up the head by the base of the rebar sticking out, and held it up so that it faced him. "You okay, Sims?"

"I don't feel any different," he said.

"Did that hurt?"

"Nothing hurts."

"Good. Jack, unfold one of those lawn chairs. Let's get him sitting up."

Jack got the chair and unfolded it, placing it next to Sims' body, lying supine on the floor.

"Can you crawl into that chair?" asked Wayne.

As if on cue, Sims' body put its palms flat on the garage floor and pushed into a sitting position, then onto its knees.

"Turn my head a little," said Sims. "I can't see."

Wayne readjusted Sims' face and the body pulled itself into the lawn chair."

"Okay," said Sims. "Finish me."

"Wayne, I did the hard part," said Jack. "Just finish it and we can tape it."

Wayne unceremoniously readjusted so that both his palms were pressed to the sides of Sims' head, and he positioned it directly over the neck. He slammed it home.

"Wayne!"

"Jeez, that was a little harder than I expected. Sorry, Sims. Looks good, though. Went right in the middle."

Jack nodded. After the initial shock of Olsen's installation method, he had to admit that it did look pretty good.

He finished it by using alcohol swabs to clean the joint and duct taping it on, using almost a quarter of a roll.

They both stood back and looked at Sims. Jack nodded. "Not bad."

"It looks like he had plastic surgery in Mexico," said Wayne.

"I'm not entering a beauty contest," said Sims. "I'm tracking down Veselov."

"Speaking of tracking," said Jack. "Let's get that knee fixed. I see you got a hatch into the attic here, Wayne. What's up there? Anything we can use?"

"Some spare ductwork, suitcases, rolls of insulation, rats, probably."

Sims' eyes lit up. "I'm hungry."

Wayne looked at him sideways, rubbing his round head. "Rats got you thinking about food?"

Sims managed a shrug. "Sorry. They sound really good right now."

"Did you like rats before?" asked Wayne, his mouth still hanging open when he finished the sentence.

"I'm starving," said Sims. "And yeah, for some reason warm, raw flesh is what I feel like I want, sick as that even sounds to me."

"Yes, I'm intentionally trying to change the subject. Sims, I'm curious. You haven't asked about your family at all. Your wife and daughter. Why not?"

"Look at me," he said. "I married up big time when I married Victoria, so you can be pretty sure she won't be mourning long. As for my Lindsay, sure. I'd like to see her, not to mention my baby boy. He was gonna be named Justin Jr., but now I wonder if that's still going to happen."

Jack watched his mouth move and listened to the gravelly voice so unlike Sims' voice in life. Uncanny. A dead man pondering his family's life without him.

"Anyway," Sims continued, "if I saw Lindsay or Victoria I'd just scare them to death, so ... no. Plus, it's not like you're just gonna let me walk away after you get what you want. I don't know where I'd go anyway."

"How the hell did this even happen?" asked Wayne.

Jack realized that Wayne's mind had been wandering in the same direction as his own; he had not stopped turning things over in his mind since he first stepped into that morgue. He was constantly retracing every step from the moment the men were killed until the present.

Jack thought back to his own activities. He had developed the photographs. They had not come out, then they had. Strange, but supernatural? Not likely. Some photographic anomaly.

"I don't know," said Jack, finally discarding his thoughts and answering Wayne's question. He reached up for the pull-down ladder rope and swung down the hatch. He unfolded the attached ladder and climbed up, stopping midway.

"Give me that hammer, would you?" he said to Wayne.

"What for?"

"You said there are rats. If Sims thinks –"

"You ain't gonna feed my officer rats."

"Hammer."

Wayne gave him the hammer. "Light's on your right."

Jack turned. "Shh. Hunting up here."

He turned and looked for a full minute without leaving the attic stairs.

"What are you doing?" asked Wayne.

"I'm fucking hunting," said Jack. "Shh."

Behind him, Jack heard Wayne say, "You ain't eatin' no goddamned rats. Not in front of me."

Jack spotted movement about eight feet away, near the large air handler for the central cooling system. He drew back his arm and let the hammer fly.

A squeal. It kept going.

"Hurry!" shouted Sims. "Before it dies!"

Jack's stomach turned again, but he'd never fed the dead before. Maybe only they knew what would satisfy them.

"Hold on," he said. He climbed into the attic and turned on the light switch. He'd hit a nice sized rat, and it twitched and jumped like Sims' body parts had in the bag. He climbed the rest of the way up the stairs and into the attic. Three knee shuffles and he was there. He snatched it by the tail.

"Heads up!" he shouted, and tossed it toward the opening. Clean shot. He heard it land on the concrete below. He continued his search and spotted the small diameter ducting. Perfect. He grabbed a two-foot length and shimmied toward the hatch.

*****

As Sims gnawed on the live rat – which wasn't alive for very long – Jack and Wayne slid the piece of ductwork up to Sims' knee and centered it. They had already used baling wire through the meatiest parts of the upper and lower legs, and wired from piece to piece all the way around. Once the duct was over all of that, they taped the ductwork to his skin, using almost half a roll.

It fit so snug that they might have worried about it cutting off Sims' circulation if he actually had some.

Sims gnawed the rat into bones before crunching the small, meaty skeleton into his mouth, chewing it perhaps five times before swallowing it.

"Not enough," he said when he was done.

"Think of something else," said Wayne. "I can't even be around that anymore."

"Let's help him up," said Jack. "I think we got it now."

They pulled Sims to his feet. He stood handily and took a few steps. "It's okay. Now let's go find Veselov."

Wayne looked at his watch. "Jesus. It's four-thirty. I have to go back to the station. I told them I had some coordination meetings to attend and for Lisa to hold my messages for me. I'm gonna need to go address some of that crap now."

"What am I supposed to do with him?" asked Jack.

"I'm an adult," said Sims.

"All due respect," said Jack, "You might as well be Frankenstein's monster. Wayne, get him some clothes first, would you?"

He was nude except for duct tape and wire.

"I'll go get him some clothes from in the house. My skinny clothes that I refused to toss. I knew there was a reason."

"Long sleeves, remember."

"That's not gonna look fuckin' weird in Florida."

"It works because we *are* in Florida," said Jack. "There are a lot of weird people here."

*****

CHAPTER FIVE

Sims had calmed a lot since first realizing his predicament, and he had stopped yelling, which was a good thing.

Jack was exhausted. "You gotta go to the station, and I need a nap before we go out. This has wiped me out."

"I get it. I'll probably need to stay until about seven o'clock or so."

"What do we do with him?" asked Jack.

"You can't tell I'm taped together," said Sims. Black goop ran down his chin.

"You're still not ready for prime time," said Wayne. "Maybe we rest up and do this tomorrow."

"He's not staying at my house."

Wayne stared at Sims. He looked at Jack and snapped his fingers. "Got it."

"What?"

"I bring a patrol car home. We lock him in the back like a perp."

131

"Perfect."

"We have to find Veselov now!" shouted Sims.

"I have some goddamned duct tape left," said Wayne. "My wife and girls are right inside that goddamned house." He pointed at the closed door. "One last time I'm telling you to keep your voice down or I'll rip you apart again and we'll continue with our original plan of weighting that bag and dumping all of you in a canal."

Jack hadn't heard of that plan, so assumed Wayne was bluffing. "Yeah," he said, mimicking Wayne's aggression. He turned to the sheriff. "Go get the squad car. I'll wait here with him."

"You sure?"

"Why?"

"Guy's dead," said Wayne. "You trust him?"

Jack stared at him. "I don't know, Jesus. Should I be worried?"

"I'm okay," said Sims. "I wouldn't hurt you."

"Fuckin' Veselov ate Kathryn Hightower, and you just ate a goddamned rat like it was KFC." He reached around to his back pocket and pulled out a pack of Zip Cuffs. "Here. We'll connect an arm and leg to the work bench."

Sims protested, but allowed it. When Wayne got back, they put Sims in the back of the patrol car and Wayne took the keys to Jack's car. They agreed Jack would drive the squad car home for the evening, because Wayne could not very well have a missing, living dead officer in the back of his car, parked at the station.

*****

Sergei Veselov stared at the carcass of Larry Peale and brought his fingers up to his nose. He breathed in. Or rather, he made the motion and tried to fill his lungs, but was not certain he actually took a breath.

No matter. He smelled no rot on his hands. They looked like they were slowly flaking away, but he could smell nothing to confirm their putrefaction. He couldn't even smell the meat of the homeowner as he chewed and swallowed his host, savoring each bite.

But it wasn't the smell or the taste; it was an instinctive knowledge that the only thing that would slow his own decay and warm his cold body was to consume warm, living flesh.

The idea of it sickened Veselov. He was used to blood, having killed his share of human beings, both men, women and children. That was not the problem.

No emotion had ever entered into murder before. There still was none. The idea of consuming human flesh sickened him, but the act did not, like an ex-smoker who despised the smell of cigarette smoke, but who, with one hit off a Marlboro, was in ecstasy again.

Eating Larry Peale was ecstasy. Sergei even got a knife from the kitchen to open him properly and scrape the meat from the bones as he snapped each one loose. He avoided the organ meat except for the heart at first; but when all the rest was gone and only bones remained, he ate them, too.

I'm a cannibal, he thought. *I would frighten even my most brutal associates.*

He had not slept, but found he was not tired. He hoped someone else would come over, for he needed more food. He had not felt full or had the need to use the toilet; as though he simply absorbed the food.

He walked into the bathroom and turned on the light.. Standing before the wall mirror, he leaned forward and studied his face.

Black scraggly lines zigged and zagged across each eye. The skin on his face was dry like desert sand. He reached up to touch it and part of his cheek powdered away. He did not remove the bandage from over the one side.

I need more flesh, he thought, looking around the bathroom. Moisturizing lotion.

He picked up the bottle of Nivea and unscrewed the cap, dumping a handful into his palm. He dipped into it with his other hand and smeared it on his face.

It soaked right in. He used more. And more.

He then took the remainder, rubbed it into both hands and spread it over his arms. It disappeared. He dumped more into his hands and spread it everywhere.

It said it was scented, but Veselov smelled nothing.

When he finished, he went into the man's closet. Ah, hats. Old men did like their hats. This man had several, but his head was not the size of Sergei's.

In the end, Sergei Veselov found a baseball cap that he was able to adjust to the maximum size and wear. It was a Florida Marlins cap.

Now to see about transportation.

*****

134

Jack Hunger sat on the sofa. The news reports had already been released that not only had Veselov's body disappeared from the morgue, but that Sims' had, too.

Jack thought about Sims' wife and the horror she must be living through. Her husband torn to pieces by a madman, now his body missing. Was this the start of something? Would whatever caused this keep on causing it?

The Pentax sat in its case on the end table. He had not taken any photographs of Kathryn Hightower, not even with his digital camera. Panic had coursed through his veins then; not work.

Watching Sims eat that rat had told him what had happened to Kathryn. Veselov had simply eaten her.

Wayne, in his role as Sheriff, had told everyone that Jack was coming down with a bad case of the flu, so nobody expected him to remain there and shoot the crime scene. They used Darius Belfour, to whom they sometimes subbed out work if Jack was away on vacation or something.

That had not happened since Jack had been with Debra. Who would he vacation with? It was fortunate that Belfour was even still willing to fill in, the work was so sparse.

The home telephone rang and his heart leapt in his chest. The only person who called him on that number was Hannah Maruska.

He got up and practically ran to the breakfast counter and grabbed the receiver off the cradle. By the time he had taken his seat once more, he had already forgotten if he had skipped or done a cartwheel back to the couch.

135

ERIC A. SHELMAN

"Hannah," he said, smiling. She had once told him that she could hear a smile in his voice when he spoke. The smile came naturally when Hannah was on the other end of the line.

"Hi," he said. "I didn't expect to hear from you so soon."

"Hi, Jack," she said, the softness of her voice sending Jack into a good place. He thought of her petite frame and the way she smelled. He would enjoy an evening of nothing but sitting on the sofa with his arm around her, feeling her warmth. That would be true peace.

Such a time had seemed so far away just before the phone rang.

"Is something wrong?" he asked.

"No, nothing. I just wanted to call and tell you that school is canceled tomorrow night. Something about a water leak in our classroom."

Jack listened, unsure how that would be important to him. Suddenly it clicked.

"Oh," he said, sure to smile so she could hear it. "Well … are you thinking we might be able to move our date up?"

"I'd like that," she said. "A date. I do not believe I have ever been on a real American date."

Thoughts ripped through Jack's mind. Veselov was out there doing God knew what. Sims was stinking up the patrol car. His car was with Olsen at the station. They would spend tonight tracking Veselov, and if they ran into trouble, they would have all day tomorrow to find him and get rid of him.

When all this was over, Veselov and hopefully, Sims, would both be dead and gone. It was an utterly bizarre situation, and if they handled it right, it would just be temporary. If he were to blow this with Hannah, he would just be alone again after life returned to normal. No way Sergei Veselov was going to mess that up.

"Jack?" her voice came, sounding unsure. "I'm sorry. I'm pressuring you."

"No, no," said Jack. "That's just crazy talk. I'm just thinking where I'll take you, and what to wear, you know, to impress you. I'm just a bit jumbled is all."

"Me, too," she said. "How was today, Jack? I hope it wasn't too difficult. I saw the news."

"Losing a fellow officer is tough on everyone," said Jack. "He had a pregnant wife and a little girl, too."

"Oh, my God, that's terrible. Well, you should get some rest, then. What time tomorrow?"

"How 'bout I'll pick you up at 7:00 tomorrow night. Anything you don't eat?"

"You choose, Jack. I will enjoy just being with you."

"Night, Hannah."

"Good night, Jack."

For that brief moment, and for several minutes after, Jack Hunger forgot about the two living dead men he would be spending time with before he met Hannah.

*****

When Olsen called at 7:00 to say he was on his way over, Jack dressed in dark clothes in preparation for the evening. He did not know where the hunt for the Russian

137

would lead, but he had to be ready. He opened the drawer beside his bed and removed his rarely used service sidearm.

It was a Glock 40. He made sure the magazine was full, and took four extras. Whether bullets would have any effect on the massive, reanimated monster, he would empty the magazine to find out.

He grabbed his keys and headed out the front door. When he got to the car he stared in disbelief.

The door was open. Sims was gone.

As he stared at the car, Olsen drove up in Jack's car, threw it in park and got out.

"Where is he?"

Jack looked at him. "I don't know, Wayne. I came out and he's gone. I don't know when or how."

"Fuck!" shouted Wayne. "I know how!"

"How?" asked Jack.

"We had a couple situations where perps turned the tables on our guys and locked them in the back of their own patrol cars. Phil Hendrickson who does the fabrication on our cars came up with a secret remote button that would open the doors. Apparently I forgot about it but Sims didn't."

"So what now?"

"It's not quite dark yet. Let's go. We need to find him, and he can't very well go too long without being noticed."

"My head keeps going back to the rat," said Jack. "Think pets in the area have anything to worry about?"

"Veselov obviously ate Kathryn Hightower," said Wayne.

"Maybe we'd better stay in the neighborhood," said Jack. "He said he was still hungry. Maybe he planned to come back all along. He knew we were going to help him find Veselov."

"Good idea. Maybe we go on foot for a while first. We see anyone gathering or gawking or something we check it out. He might draw some eyes."

The men took opposite sides of the street, walking slowly. The sun had begun to sink, but would not be entirely down until after 8:00 or so. Visibility in between the houses was pretty good.

It did not take twenty-five minutes before the scream sent both men running.

*****

Jack and Wayne charged between the beige, 2-story home and the lime green ranch style home. The low, chain-link fence was only four feet tall, so both men were able to vault over it with one arm on the top of the rail.

Sims was down on all fours. His face was buried in a bloody, shredded carcass and the screaming came from an open window just behind Wayne.

"Jack, show her your badge and calm her down. I don't want to look her way because if she sees the Sheriff here, she'll tell everyone. Hurry."

Jack spun around and went to the window. He had his wallet in his hand and showed her his badge.

"Ma'am, quiet, please!" he said.

She closed her mouth and burst into tears. "Thank God!" she shouted.

He turned. "You got this? I need to go inside."

139

"Got it, got it," said Wayne. "Do what you have to to keep her quiet," said Wayne.

At first Jack's mind thought Wayne meant to kill her. He wasn't certain what else would shut her up after seeing a man eating her beloved pet – whatever kind of pet it had been – but he would think of something.

He went to the back screen door and the woman came out to meet him. She peered around the corner of the house to see, but Jack put a hand on her shoulder and nudged her back toward the door. "C'mon, ma'am. You don't need to see that."

"What is it? What is that man doing? Is he insane?"

Jack's mind clicked. "What's your name?"

"Alice Cleary," she said.

"Well, Ms. Cleary, he is. He escaped from an overturned transport vehicle. He was being moved from one location to another, and the van was in an accident. The lock popped and he's been out for a few hours. That's why we were in the area."

"I didn't see anything about it on the news," she said, tearfully. "My poor Roscoe."

"Roscoe's your ..."

"My standard poodle," she said.

That explained to Jack why he hadn't been sure it wasn't a black sheep. He hadn't connected poodle fur with a dog.

"I know he's irreplaceable," said Jack. "But we need you to keep this to yourself. Are your neighbors typically home now?" Jack was worried that her screams were heard by others.

She shook her head. "No, they're seasonal. Up in Nebraska and New Jersey now."

"Good. We've got him now and we can secure him. I know we can't bring Roscoe back, and for that I'm sorry. We can give you enough to buy a new dog. I know that sounds cold, but it's all we can do for you."

She sobbed, shaking her head.

"Ms. Cleary?"

"He was sick. Old, too. I've been with him fourteen years. I've been thinking about putting him down, but ... not like this. My God."

Jack put his arm around Alice Cleary. "I know. It's hard. I'm sorry. Will you be okay?"

"Take him away, please?"

"The man?"

"Roscoe," she said. "I can't deal with that. Take him."

"Do you want his collar and tags?"

"Yes, please."

"Okay. I'll bring them in. Do you have a ... garbage bag? We weren't prepared for this right now."

She nodded.

"Okay. Stay in the house. I'm going to get our squad car and my partner will stay outside with him until I get back."

*****

Sergei Veselov found the keys to the car easily enough; they hung on a small rack by the door, carved out of wood and shaped like a key. He lifted the Lincoln key from the brass hook and carried it into the garage.

141

As he stood looking at the black Lincoln Town Car, it occurred to him that while he had felt drawn in a direction, he actually had no idea where he was going. That would make it impossible. He got inside anyway, closing the door and sitting in the plush, leather bucket seat.

He gripped the wheel and analyzed his senses.

Two directions. He was being torn in two directions. Both took him westward, but one pulled him to the north and the other pulled him to the south. He felt he should understand these opposing draws, but he did not.

Veselov shivered. He put his hand up to his face, laying his flat palm on his right cheek.

The warmth he had gained from Peale's body was leaving him, and with its passing, Sergei felt weak and aching for more.

He needed to know more; the exact place where he was being pulled. He closed his eyes.

A vision swirled there, a picture. It moved, like a movie behind his eyes, swimming in and out of focus. A boy and a girl on the couch with their mother between them. On the other sofa, a man.

The man.

The tin man. His killer.

Sergei felt he was there, in the room with them. He looked down at his legs and took a step, then another and another. As he did so, the couple and their children fell behind him. He moved to the front door of their house.

He reached out his hand and tried to grip the doorknob, but he passed through it. He then stepped through the solid door and found himself on the porch.

142

With several more steps, he walked down the concrete walkway and into the street, arriving there in a split second, as though floating over the surface. Stopping to study the street in both directions, he saw an intersection half a block away.

Sergei decided that was where he needed to be and in another fraction of a second he had floated there as well. He stared up at the street signs. Canal Street and SW 47th Avenue.

He floated back and stared at the street number of SWAT Team member Derek Williams' home.

Sergei felt a strange, blissful satisfaction when he again found himself sitting within the confines of the Lincoln. He turned on the key and powered up the GPS. In it, he entered 4742 SW 47th Avenue.

It said it was located in Cape Coral, and that he would be there in thirty-four minutes.

Sergei was not sure he could go that long without eating.

*****

After they got Sims back to the car and Wayne removed the fuse plug that allowed the emergency unlock in the back seat to function, both men turned in their seats, the car idling.

"Sims, what the hell were you thinking?"

"I didn't mind it in the car," he said. "It was warm. I'm cold. That's why. It's warm ... I'm warm, just not on the inside."

"So eating a poodle alive is the answer?" asked Jack.

143

"It was meat," gurgled Sims. "If you knew how sharp I feel now, you'd find me another."

Jack looked at Wayne and turned again. "What do you mean, sharp?"

"I can sense the Russian."

"So where is he?" asked Olsen.

"West of here," said Sims. "Across the river."

"Can you pinpoint it any better than that?" asked Wayne. "I mean, we can't just drive every street of a 115 square mile city until we find him."

"Get me more food, get me warmed up. I need to enhance my brain function with protein," said Sims.

Wayne turned on the heater, spinning the fan control to full.

"Not external," said Sims. "I need to be warmed from the inside. I need fresh meat. I think you know that."

"I might be avoiding thinking about it," said Wayne, pulling the car down the street and making a U-turn.

Jack turned to look at Sims. He was smiling, as though he had told a joke, and Jack found the smile of the dead officer to be chilling. He forced himself to watch Sims' face and asked, "Officer Sims, why are you drawn to Veselov?"

Sims's smile broadened and he closed his black-veined eyes, jaundiced to a pure yellow that almost had a light of their own. His eyes opened and he stared into those of Jack Hunger. "Because he ended my life."

He ended my life. The words rang in Jack's ears. He slapped Wayne in the arm.

"What's the name of the SWAT guy who killed Veselov?" he asked.

144

"Why?"

"Because that's where Veselov is headed."

"How do you know?"

"Because Sims is drawn to Veselov for the same reason; he's his killer."

"His name is Derek Williams. Are you sure?"

"Hell no, I'm not sure," said Jack. "But it makes sense, right? I mean, none of this makes sense, but in this entire realm of senselessness, this fits perfectly."

"I don't know where he lives," said Wayne.

"And you can't tap into it in this computer here?"

The police laptop mounted in the bracket was dark. "This one quit working, which is why I took this car."

"So look it up on your phone."

"You know cop's addresses aren't available on the tax roles," said Wayne. "Only way is for me to connect into the Sheriff's Office database. You can't do that from a mobile device. Safety precaution."

"My house, then. I'm pretty sure you know where that is."

*****

"I want to come in," said Sims, when Olsen parked the car.

"No way" said Jack. "You can wait here."

"I'm drawn there," insisted Sims.

"Why the fuck would you be drawn to my house? Don't even think about my house," said Jack. "We're going in for two minutes and we'll be back out." Jack turned to look at Sims and saw black liquid running from his ears and eyes, as well as the corners of his mouth.

145

When he spoke, the inky-black liquid ran down, badly staining the front of his shirt where blood and gore from the devoured dog also resided.

Jack felt sick. He opened the door and got out. A moment later, the other door slammed. He stared at nothing and felt a hand pat him on the shoulder. "You okay, man?"

"No," said Jack. "I finally … finally, after all this time, I get the nerve to ask Hannah out, and all this shit happens. She's amazing. I'm – well, I'm not amazing. In the scope of everything I'm sure that doesn't seem like a big deal to you, but I have a date with her tomorrow night, and come hell or high water, I'm going to be on it."

"We're doing this tonight, Jack," said Wayne. "Finishing it. If you still feel like it, you should be able to go on your date."

"Wayne, did you see Sims just now? The black stuff? His smile? He's looking forward to something, and whatever it is, it's a standoff or whatever that I don't really want to be around for. In fact, I'd like for all of this shit to play out without me."

Olsen dropped his hands to his sides. "You don't think I feel the same?" He looked at his watch. "It's dark. It's 8:45. We follow this guy's lead or your hunch or whatever, and we have this all over with by 1:00 in the morning. That's if we decide to get rid of the bodies, 'cause that'll take some time."

"Let's go, then."

"Jack?"

"Yeah?"

"Why does Sims want to come inside your house?"

"I wish I knew, but he's not."

"Does *he* know?"

"He hasn't said."

"I hate his voice. Sounds like a voice from the grave."

"It kind of is," said Jack. "He just never made it there."

"Yet," said Olsen.

Yet, Jack hoped.

*****

Sergei Veselov pushed the garage door opener button and reversed the Town Car from the garage. When he was clear, he pushed the button again, closing it.

"Turn right on Victoria Avenue," the electronic voice commanded.

Sergei eased the car to a stop at the corner and followed the verbal instructions. He was advised to turn right on US-41, which he did.

Now he was on the street also known as Tamiami Trail, which ran north and south. He had never been in the area, but the map image on the GPS was set to display north as up, and he was driving north.

An alert sounded on the dashboard.

LOW FUEL.

Sergei closed his eyes. If anything else could slow him down, it seemed that it would. He scanned the roadway for a petrol station until he spotted a Racetrack on his right about a quarter mile away.

He turned into the driveway, but did not pull up to a pump. In order to pay with the cash he had taken from Peale, he would have to go in and pre-pay.

Instead, he eyed the other two patrons. One was a woman in her twenties, dark, almost black hair. She wore a short, leather skirt that came to just below where her shaved pussy would be, Veselov thought.

Despite his time in prison, he did not envision himself having sex with her. In his mind's eye, he was biting and tearing her vagina away from her body in one fleshy mouthful, the warm blood and tissue giving him strength.

He pulled up and parked on the other side of the pump from which she filled the tank of her Toyota.

He unrolled his window. "Miss," he said, trying to force his voice to sound friendly and inviting. "I am disabled, and have got cash. Would you be so kind as to let me give you the money and allow me to fill my tank from your pump?"

"Excuse me?" she asked, leaning around to see him. Veselov kept his eyes facing away from her and only the top of the window cracked, and he knew from the bright glare of the halogen lighting that she could not make out his face through the glass.

He held three twenty-dollar bills through the crack. She did not take them.

"Sorry," she said. "I'd like to help, but those could be fake and my parents only charge my card up once a month."

She finished pumping, put the nozzle back in the pump stand and screwed on her gas cap, closing the hinged door.

Sergei felt a surge of hunger and rage. He fired the engine and forced himself to ease the car from the aisle rather than floor the accelerator and spin the tires until they got so hot they burst into flames.

He drove around the entire bank of pumps and pulled directly in front of the light green Corolla, throwing it in park. He casually unplugged the GPS and released the suction cup, pulling it down.

The Corolla honked. She could have backed up, but this told Sergei how stupid the American girl was. He opened his door and walked toward her car. Her window was down and when she saw him up close, she gasped.

He grabbed her throat and squeezed. Something there snapped, and he knew he had pressed too hard with his fingers. She was still alive for now. He reached down and opened the door. Unsnapping her seatbelt, he leaned forward and lifted her under her legs and fed her body over the front seats and dumped her limp frame into the back.

With that, Sergei Veselov dropped into the driver's seat and shifted the already running Corolla into reverse. He backed all the way to the driveway, saw it was clear, backed onto Tamiami Trail and continued North.

He stopped five minutes later as he heard the girl's breathing grow shallower.

She *must* be alive when he sought nourishment.

*****

149

CHAPTER SIX

Inside the house, Wayne tapped on the computer keys and accessed the Sheriff's department database. He found the name of the officer and selected it.

"Okay. Got a pen?"

"I'm ready, but you should just hit print," said Jack.

"Smartass."

"Better'n being a dumbass like you."

"Jesus, Jack, I'm your fuckin' boss. I'm everyone's boss."

"So fire me," said Jack, smiling for the first time all evening. They could be on the golf course smoking cigars, or at the bowling alley tossing back a pitcher of beer. It was what Jack wished they were doing. This was what they did and they were best friends.

It was the only way it would work, Jack knew. The trust they had in one another at that very moment was perhaps greater than any confidence any two people had ever shared.

What they faced was terrifying.

Wayne got up. "Let's go. Get your gun."

Jack lifted his light jacket. "Got it. I've had it all night."

"Good man. Let's go."

"He wants to go somewhere else," said Jack. "We need to hear him out."

"I'm open to it," said Olsen. "He's kind of extraordinary. Wouldn't surprise me he might have some connection to him."

"Nothing will ever surprise me again," said Jack. "It might scare the shit out of me or fry my brain, but it won't surprise me. Now let's go. I think we're stalling."

Wayne went to the door and opened it. "Ain't no foolin' you, my friend."

*****

Back in the car, both men turned to Sims. He looked from one to the other. "What?"

"You ready?"

"Yeah," he answered. "I have an address."

"An address? So do we," said Wayne.

"What is it?" asked Sims. "Is it 2255 Aldridge Street?"

"In the Cape?" asked Olsen.

"No. I don't think so. In Fort Myers."

"Good, 'cause there isn't an Aldridge Street in the Cape. We're going to 47th first."

"You have to go to Aldridge!" shouted Sims. "He's there! I saw him there behind my eyes."

"Behind what?" asked Jack.

151

"I closed my eyes. He was standing there, in the kitchen, reaching for something. Keys maybe."

"If you were in the kitchen, how do you know the address?" asked Wayne.

"I saw a letter on the counter. I could touch it and I picked it up and read the address. You have to go!"

"Man, you're still a cop at heart," said Wayne. "Can he do this stuff too, Sims?"

"Who? What?"

"The Russian. Can he look at shit behind his eyes. Like see us chasing him."

"How would I know? It's not like I'm suddenly an expert on reanimated corpses! Now hurry before you miss him!"

The southernmost bridge in Cape Coral fed into south Fort Myers. If Veselov was where Sims thought, it would be the fastest way there. If they went to 47th first and he wasn't there, it might be too late to find him.

Wayne threw the transmission into drive, hit his lights and siren, and drove toward Cape Coral Parkway.

Traffic on the bridge was light. He zigzagged through the cars, hoping he would not encounter another cop until he crossed into Fort Myers. He did not have any jurisdiction in the Cape, and he damned sure wasn't supposed to be running his lights and siren until he was on his own turf.

*****

Fifteen minutes later, they pulled up in front of a pink house with blue shutters. The address was 2255

Aldridge Street. Wayne drove the car three more houses down before pulling it to the curb and cutting the engine.

"Let's go! Hurry!" shouted Sims, his excitement bubbling over; the black muck running from his chin, eyes and ears.

Jack hated to think what other orifices leaked the stuff.

"We do this smart," said Wayne. "We all know what he did to you, Sims."

"Thanks for the reminder."

"No, no. Thank you," said Jack. "We get to stare at you all night."

"I'll fucking trade you," said Sims.

"Good point," said Wayne. "Apologize, Jack."

"Are your feelings hurt?" asked Jack.

"Not really," gurgled Sims. "Don't really have them anymore. I'm hungry and I want to kill Veselov. There's something else, but it's not priority for some reason, and I can't pinpoint it."

When he said the Ps in pinpoint, black muck spattered both men through the metal cage and they both wiped their faces.

"Sorry," said Sims.

"Are you?" asked Jack.

Sims shook his head. "No."

"Brutally fuckin' honest aren't you, sweetheart?" said Wayne, opening his door, then stopping. He looked back at Sims. "If we let you come in, will you promise not to run?"

"Run?" said Sims. "Killing that son of a bitch is all I want to do. For now."

153

"Jeez, Sims," said Jack. "Can't you just pretend this is done and look beyond that? Maybe the thing you've gotta do next is about self-preservation. Maybe you want to kill us and you don't even know it yet."

"I don't care about me," he said. "I care about eating and I care about killing Veselov for now. That's it."

Jack opened his door and went around to let Sims out. When he got out of the car, he and Jack walked around and met Wayne on the sidewalk.

"Jack, you still got your shield?" asked Wayne.

"Duh. I carry it in my wallet 24/7."

"Okay, hang it off your pocket. If anyone sees us, I want them to get the hell back indoors and know we're keeping their neighborhood safe is all."

"Good idea," said Jack. "Split up?"

"Yeah. You go around the left side and I'll go around to the right. Listen, then check windows, but only the ones you can fit through. If you find one unlocked, come get me."

"You do the same."

"I knew that. Who's Sims going with?"

"He can come with me," said Wayne.

"See you in a minute," said Jack.

Jack ducked down and ran across the lawn. He did not know whether a family of five lived in the house or a single mom. Or Veselov. Maybe now it was Veselov, all alone.

*****

154

On the side of the house, Jack found no windows to be either partially open or unlocked. He was in the back yard within two and a half minutes and saw Olsen rounding the corner with Sims.

"Sims says he's gone."

"How the hell does he know that?"

"I'll go in and look," said Sims. "What have I got to lose?"

Jack looked at Wayne. "He's a big bastard. Sims, you think you can take him?"

"Give me your gun?"

"Not a chance."

"Wait," said Wayne. "You still remember your firearms training?"

Olsen was a stickler for good training, and Jack remembered he had trained Sims at the range.

"I'd show you, but I imagine you want me to wait until the need arises."

"Exactly," said Olsen. "Jack, give him your gun."

"*My* gun?"

"I'm better with my gun than you are with yours, so give him your gun and let's put this to rest."

Jack gave Sims the Glock 40. "Don't shoot unless you have to."

Sims took it and walked toward the rear sliding glass door. No dogs barked. He tried the door.

It slid open. He went inside.

Jack and Wayne watched, keeping an eye out in case someone was watching them.

*****

Sergei felt strong. He leaned to his right, reaching over the carcass of the girl's ravaged body, and pulled on the door handle of the car. The inside panel ripped from the door like tissue paper. He released it and raised his arms, pushing upward against the roof of the Toyota with his balled fists. Two dents formed instantly, but if he had continued pressing, he knew his power would split the steel.

The girl had been good nourishment. Youth. When he'd eaten the old man, it had been good, but not like this. He felt fifty times as strong as before.

Maybe even a hundredfold more powerful.

He eased the car to a stop, parking it in front of a vacant lot two houses down from Williams'.

He got out of the car and walked toward the house. He was invincible now. It was the perfect time to strike.

*****

Derek Williams looked at the clock as he tucked his seven-year-old daughter, Sabrina, into bed. She had insisted on staying up until 10:00, and for the first time in her young life, he had relented.

Darrin, who was nine years old, wasn't interested in saying up until 10:00. He had nodded off quite a bit earlier and Derek had put him to bed in the top bunk of their shared bedroom at 9:00.

As he always did for his little girl, he hummed quietly as he tucked the covers around her, pulling the switch on her lamp to turn on the black light. It was the perfect nightlight for her, because it wasn't bright, but she could still see.

Above them both, Darrin snored away, ever the sound sleeper.

Sabrina rolled over as Derek finished humming the last note to Van Morrison's *Crazy Love*. She didn't know what the song was, but Sabrina seemed to like it and she was always out before he reached the end.

He pulled the door closed, ran a hand through his blonde, short-cropped hair and dropped down beside Kelly.

"Just us again," he said.

"I know. Our one hour alone."

He looked at her. "It's worth it, right? They're so smart. You're doing a great job with them. I can't believe you weren't a teacher when I met you."

She snuggled in to him. "Okay, enough about me. I think you've only got like seven more episodes of Californication left," said Kelly. "Better get your fill of tits and ass besides mine while the kids are in bed."

"I know," he said, rubbing her arm. "I'm gonna miss seeing nice tits when this series is over."

She slapped him and smiled, leaning away from him and grabbing the bottom of her blouse and pulling it over her head, exposing her breasts.

"Hey babe, would you make me a plate of Ritz crackers and cheese?" he asked, staring at the TV and pretending not to notice.

"Screw you," she said, pulling her top back down. "You won't be seeing these girls again anytime soon."

He laughed. "I'm kidding you. Show them to me again. C'mon, I'll give them the proper appreciation."

Kelly smiled and shook her head as she pressed the remote and started the show.

157

As the final note of the opening theme song played, the front door burst in.

Derek whirled around, reaching for the side table to grab his pistol.

In the middle of his reach, fright overtook him and he froze, his brain locked up. It was impossible. The thing running toward him, already three giant steps into his living room with perhaps only one to go, was the Russian.

It was Sergei Veselov; the man he had killed yesterday.

His momentum carried him to the Sig Sauer and his fingers wrapped around the grip. He went over the edge of the couch and hit the ground firing.

*****

"Did Veselov do this?" asked Wayne.

"You really need to ask?" asked Jack, answering his question with a question.

"He … he ate all the best parts," said Sims, kneeling down beside the ravaged carcass.

Jack looked at the sheriff. "I have a feeling this goes way beyond rats and dogs."

"If you could see the chill running down my back you'd fire on it," said Olsen.

Sims started to reach into the nearly empty cavity when Wayne kicked his arm.

"Get the hell away from there, Sims!" he shouted.

"I need it," he said. "I'm weak."

"You got poodle in you from like half an hour ago," said Jack. "That's really going to have to do for now."

"You don't know!" cried Sims, more black stuff coming from his mouth. "I can feel him, but I can't think if I don't have food!"

"I'll check the goddamned freezer," said Wayne.

"That's not what I need. I know what I need."

Jack rubbed his head and took three steps away from Sims and the body on the floor. It wasn't possible to tell whether it was a man or woman because almost all of it was gone. Judging from the pajamas, it was likely a man, but at first glance it was just shredded, blood-soaked flannel and bone with some meat clinging to it.

"We have an address. We need to go," said Olsen.

"I thought we should go there first," said Jack. "If you remember."

"Yeah, yeah," said Wayne. "Too late for this guy."

"If you'd have moved your asses when I said, we might have made it here on time."

"Well, somebody had to eat a fuckin' poodle, and it wasn't me. Let's go then."

Sims suddenly pushed off his knees and grabbed Wayne's right leg. He opened his mouth and chomped down hard."

"Fuck!" shouted Olsen, trying to jerk his leg away. He lost his balance and toppled backward, his head smacking the sliding glass door.

Wayne was out and Sims was doubling down with no resistance coming from Olsen.

"Sims!" shouted Jack, reaching for his gun that was no longer there. He looked and saw it on the floor beside Sims, who was singularly focused on Wayne Olsen's leg. Sims growled and tore clean through Olsen's pants, tearing out a hunk of calf meat.

Jack leapt off his feet, flying over the four feet of distance between him and the attacking Sims.

He landed atop the reanimated corpse, expecting that his sheer momentum would detach Sims, but the dead officer gripped tightly to Olsen's leg and chewed veraciously. The pain apparently woke Olsen up, whose scream pierced the night as his eyes opened wide.

Olsen managed to grab his service weapon, and he screamed, "Jack! Move! Get the hell off him!"

Jack twisted off to his right and scrambled out the bedroom door, grabbing his gun from the floor on the way. He rolled onto his stomach and assumed firing position, aiming dead at Sims midsection.

As Jack cleared Sims' body, Wayne fired into the officer, a cloud of black mist spattering the wall behind him. The explosion sounded louder to Jack than it probably was, but he fully realized that he and Wayne had no idea what had happened earlier, and what kind of noise had been made when Veselov killed the occupant of the house. The police could've been called any number of minutes before their arrival.

Sims had been knocked clean of Olsen's leg, but now he scrambled back toward him. Jack jumped to his feet and kicked Sims in the head, feeling it shift slightly under his foot.

"Stay the fuck back, Sims!" Olsen screamed, his face twisted with pain. "We'll tear your ass apart again and burn you!" He fired into Sims' midsection again, the jolt twisting the officer's body sideways.

Jack scrambled to his feet and held the gun on Sims, his entire body shaking. Sims stared up at him in the semi-darkness and put up a hand. "Okay, okay! I was out of control. I need food. This isn't my fault."

Jack stared at him, disbelieving. It *wasn't* his fault, but that didn't matter. He was already dead. Jack wouldn't have too much of a problem making him dead again.

"What the hell is that stuff leaking out of you?"

"I don't have any idea. You shot me, which is the only reason it is coming out."

"It's not blood."

"Sorry," said Sims.

"It looks like ink. Exactly like ink. I've thought that since I first saw it in the morgue," said Jack.

"I don't think it would be that," said Sims, but again the dark shadow passed behind his eyes and he did not look at Jack.

The thought nagged at the back of Jack's mind, and there seemed to be some connection somewhere, but damned if he could stretch far enough to string them together.

"Pardon me," said Wayne, still on the floor.

"Sorry, man," said Jack. "Get up, Sims, slowly. Wayne, you okay?"

"Fuckin' leg's bleeding like a stuck pig," he said. "I think he tore a tendon."

"We're gonna have to use our remedial first aid training to fix you up, because if Veselov is anything like the good guy here is, we've got bigger trouble than we ever thought."

Olsen nodded. "Here," he said, holding out the cuffs.

Jack leaned over to take them, then held out a hand. "Here." Olsen took his hand and Jack pulled him up, never taking his eyes off Sims.

"Turn the fuck around," said Olsen, breathing hard.

Jack thought it was strange to see Sims get to his feet without seeming winded at all. It had been quite a struggle. It just drove home how dead Sims really was.

Sims obeyed, putting his hands instinctively behind his back. "I'm sorry, Sheriff Olsen. You don't even know. It was like I was a cartoon wolf and you were a cartoon steak. I couldn't stop myself."

"Next time you fucking pretend you're in a goddamned Archie and Veronica comic."

"Can you bandage that yourself?" asked Jack. "I need to keep my gun on him."

"Is he okay?" asked Wayne.

Jack looked at Sims. "Well, I don't know why he cares, but are you?"

"Because it was a shitload of work putting him together," said Wayne.. "For all that, this bastard's going to find Veselov for us."

"Yeah," said Jack. "You were wrong bringing us here. No telling where the Russian is now."

"If you believe the address you have is of the officer who killed him, it's the right place to go," said Sims.

"Let's get you bandaged up, Wayne. Next time he stays in the car."

*****

Sergei Veselov felt the liquid running from the bullet wounds and down his body. He had not felt any

162

surface stimulation before, so the sensation was new; it had been numb. Since he had consumed the young girl he had abducted from the petrol station, his senses and his strength had multiplied.

When Williams' magazine was empty, Sergei moved toward him and kicked the highly trained officer in the head, riding him down until his head impacted the floor.

Beside him, the woman's piercing scream needled its way into his head and he reached over with one powerful hand and punched her into unconsciousness.

A sound from his left. He turned.

It was a little boy. Veselov watched the child watching him, and said, "Come here, young man."

The boy did not. His eyes were large and frightened. He had medium-length brown hair and big eyes that looked blue in the light from the living room.

Veselov looked again at the cop. This was why he was here. He would make the man pay for his crime.

His entire family would suffer while Veselov became stronger.

*****

"I don't know if I can move. It's throbbing."

"I need something to eat," said Sims.

"Don't even start," said Olsen.

"Can you check the freezer? See if there's any raw meat or anything? I can't help what I feel and I can't control myself."

Sims looked regretful, but Jack wasn't sure if it was an act or what. "I'm not so sure now," he said. "If you gain strength when you eat, we don't need you any stronger."

"Yeah," said Wayne. "If he can't die, then I'm fine with him getting weaker."

"So what do you think kills you?" asked Jack.

"What? Me?" asked Sims, who sat in a wooden kitchen chair from the 1970s, most likely.

"No, your fuckin' twin brother over there," said Olsen. "Yeah, you."

A shadow passed behind Sims' eyes and Jack saw the expression come and disappear. "What, Sims? What are you hiding?"

"Nothing. If you don't go, I think you're going to find it's too late again."

Jack stood. "Wayne, he's right. I can't believe the cops didn't come yet."

Wayne said, "Go tap on that window. I think I know why. When we were checking the outside, I tapped on a few. It's double-paned, hurricane glass."

Jack went to the window and banged on it with the side of his balled fist. "Yeah, it is. Almost soundproof."

"There's one thing that turned out our way tonight," said Wayne.

"Don't get used to it," said Jack.

Sirens sounded in the distance. Jack looked at Olsen. "We speak too soon?"

"Maybe," said Wayne. "Help me up."

Jack gave him an arm and he pulled himself out of the chair. "Back door, Wayne. Sims, c'mon. Get up and let's move."

The three hurried to the slider as the lights flashed against the front shades. When they were through the slider, Jack pulled it closed.

They slipped into the night, working their way to the north until they reached a fence covered with twisting, turning vines. It looked like Star Jasmine, and it was two feet thick.

"Get over it as fast as you can. Sims, here," said Jack, interlacing his hands. "Step into this and just get the hell over. I'm not uncuffing you."

Flashlights shone inside the house now, throwing white trails across the back curtains.

Sims stepped into his hand and Jack boosted him over. He landed with a thump on the other side.

"Now you, Wayne. Hurry."

"I can do it."

"Hurry," he whispered. Olsen relented and stepped into his makeshift stirrup. Jack strained to push Olsen up high enough. He disappeared over the fence.

The slider opened and Jack tucked himself behind the bushes. The flashlight shone onto the back yard and hit the fence just two feet to his right. Jack looked down and saw his legs were exposed.

The light moved by him. Six feet away, now toward the house. The officer in the door turned and Jack clearly heard him yell, "Rollins, get two guys out here to search this back yard!"

He went back inside. The boost of energy Jack felt surged through his arms and he flew over that fence as though he were a pole vaulter in the Olympics.

When he landed, Olsen was there, helping him to his feet.

Sims stood just three feet away. He was unsteady on his feet and he stared into the night.

"I think he's telling the truth," said Olsen. "He's getting weaker. We're gonna need to get him something to eat if we still think he's of value."

"If we miss Veselov at Williams' house, he will be."

"Then we should just get there," said Sims. "I'm sorry."

"C'mon," said Jack, leading the way across the lawn. "Stay as far from the houses as you can."

The fence had been for the house where Veselov had done his damage; there was no fence separating the next door neighbor's home from the one beside it. The men ran into the next yard.

A metallic sound came suddenly, and a deep bark accompanied it. A figure ran out of the shadows of the house, and Jack realized the sound of metal was the dog's chain clinking against itself.

Jack looked, but he could not tell where the dog was chained. If it were done to give the dog access to the entire yard, they could be in trouble.

"Go, go!" whispered Jack.

They all moved as fast as they could. The light came on in the house and now suddenly all three men were illuminated as they reached the north property line and charged between the homes toward the street.

The dog was caught short-chained, and spun around by his neck, its barking cut off with a squeal.

Wayne hobbled along, but maintained more speed than Jack thought he would be able to manage. They charged into the front lawn of the next house and Jack glanced back to see the officers were completely focused on the crime scene.

"Stop," he said, crouching down.

Olsen stood beside him, unable to crouch. He bent as low as he could.

"Okay ... just a minute. I left it unlocked, so no alarm chirp."

"Can you see?"

"Yeah," said Jack. "They're moving to the side yard now."

"This street connects with Katy Street at the end," said Wayne. "Now I wish we hadn't drove a cruiser here."

"We could just hit the lights like we got another call," said Jack.

"Or fire it up and just sneak our way out," said Wayne. "If they see me, I'm fucked."

"Yeah, never mind about Sims."

They got to the car and slipped inside after the officers pulled their crime scene tape around a tree and worked their way between the houses.

"Fire it and drive," said Wayne. "Leave the headlights off."

"Because that won't look suspicious at all," said Sims.

"Were you this much of a smartass when you were alive, Sims?" asked Wayne.

Jack didn't expect that Sims would answer and sure enough, no snide reply came from the dead rookie cop.

Jack turned the key and the motor came to life. He left the lights off initially, putting the car in gear and idling toward the intersection.

As he approached the stop sign, he turned on the headlights and turn signal. It would not do for the officers down the street to see a police car appear to be sneaking from the scene.

They turned West on Katy.

Jack eyed the dashboard clock. It was just after 11:00 PM.

They had wasted almost an hour there. No telling what kind of carnage the Russian could reap in that amount of time.

*****

CHAPTER SEVEN

There had been a six-pack of duct tape rolls in the garage. Sergei used it effectively on the unconscious cop and his wife's hands and wrists, with a piece over their mouths just in case.

The boy had given his name as Darrin. He told Veselov his sister's name was Sabrina. The boy had been extremely frightened at the appearance of Sergei's face, but he merely told the boy that he was dressed up for a costume party and was going as a zombie.

Lying to children was so effortless and easy; they would believe anything. Little Darrin did not need to maintain his belief for long.

Sergei came out of the kids' bedroom, hearing the uncontrollable whimpers of Sabrina behind him. She had been in the bottom bunk and Darrin on the top. Sergei had warned her not to peek, but it was now apparent that she had.

Sergei placed the treasured item in his hand on the end table by the couch, shoved the woman's legs aside and sat.

Sergei had neither the desire nor the intention to delay the death of Derek Williams. The specially trained tin man was the pig who had executed him, and his flesh would warm and sustain Veselov. As repulsed by his own desire for human flesh as he had initially been, the mere thought of sinking his teeth into it and feeling the warm blood flow across his teeth and tongue now made him dizzy with anticipation.

Would it always be this way? Was this to be his pursuit now, or would he one day absorb enough human flesh and life force that he would be self-sustaining?

The members of Krovozhadnost would at first be surprised, then perhaps horrified. The moment he made a production of removing his clothing and his former family witnessed the massive injuries Veselov had survived, they would respect him; they would know he was the natural choice to lead them.

Those who could not be led would be torn apart and devoured. Even if he should reach the point where he did not need their flesh to become stronger, he would still savor each bite, the act of which would force any members of the family to submit to his immortality and answer only to him.

The SWAT officer's wife lay beside him on the sofa, unconscious, with an angry bruise forming above her right cheekbone. She was still breathing, so no rush to consume her before she died. She wasn't even close.

Sergei was not in a hurry now. Nobody even knew he was alive. If the cops made a statement, it would say

170

nothing other than his body was stolen from the morgue; there would be no BOLOs or APBs out on Sergei Veselov; he was a dead man.

That was good. It would take him all night to do what he needed to do here, and that was fine. It was all part of the plan, impromptu as it was.

*****

Williams awoke and realized his mouth was taped and his head hurt badly. His vision was blurred as his eyes searched the room.

He found himself on his back on the floor behind the sofa. He looked to his left and saw the bald head of the big Russian. He was sitting on the sofa facing away from him. Kelly had been sitting there before he was knocked out.

"Mmmm!" he said, and Veselov turned toward him. He smiled when he turned, and the face that stared at him was horrific. He immediately thought of Darrin and Sabrina. *Where were they? Were they alive?*

"Mmmmmmm!" he moaned, his eyes flashing as much intensity as he could muster. "Mmm Mmmm!"

"You must learn to articulate, officer Williams," said Veselov, a hint of cheerfulness in his tone.

The killer rose from his seat on the sofa with more ease than a man of the Russian's size and injuries should have been able to muster.

He's dead. He is dead. I know a kill and he was so dead.

171

The man, still smiling, looked at Williams before reaching down and lifting Kelly into the air so that Williams could see her.

"Mmm mmm mmmm!" shouted Williams.

"What is that? Put her down?"

Veselov threw Kelly's body across the room as though she weighed nothing and Derek's wife slammed off the wall of the dining room, her body crumpling to the floor. The framed oil painting that hung on the wall there came off its hanger, landing atop her before sliding away.

Kelly awakened and moaned. Relief washed over Derek's body as he saw her eyes open and heard her whimper beneath her own duct taped mouth.

He almost tried to get her attention, but chose not to. The moment she saw he was also incapacitated she might panic, which would not do anybody any good.

Tears sprung from his eyes as he stared at his wife.

Veselov strode over to her and reached down, snatching her from the floor as if she weighed no more than a puppy. He carried her easily back to the sofa and dropped her onto it again, out of Williams' sight.

She was alive. He wondered about his children. He prayed, his eyes squeezed closed. He needed a miracle.

*****

Sabrina wanted her mommy and daddy.

Her brother had gotten up to leave the room a while earlier and it had woken her up. She guessed she had fallen asleep again, but later on there was another sound that woke her up again.

When she opened her eyes, Sabrina saw a big man walking Darrin back into their room, holding him by the hand. He led her older brother to the bed and lifted him to the top bunk, over her head.

When she first heard Darrin scream, she began crying. Just seconds after, her older brother's screaming became muffled, then stopped. She could not control her whimpering, and in a flash, the man was down there, touching her with hands that were slick and wet and smelled funny. She heard a sound and something tearing, and his big wet hand was sticking something over her mouth.

Her nose was stuffy and she was having trouble breathing, but she forced herself to be calm. Her mommy and daddy would say for her to take slow, deep breaths if they thought she was panicking, which she felt like she was now.

After taping her mouth, she heard the strange sound and tear again, and this time the man taped her hands and feet together. When he was finished, she lay there, watching him stand beside her bed and do something to Darrin.

It sounded like a big dog eating. Or licking. She did not know which it was and did not want to know. He grunted and groaned once in a while, and tears squirted through her clenched eyes.

Her eyes fell to the clock on her nightstand. She watched as almost thirty minutes passed while he stood there, doing something to her brother, who no longer made any sounds. Tears leaked from her eyes as she tried to stop her own shaking.

Then he walked away from the bed and stopped. He turned in the semi-darkness, some spots glowing on his hands and arms and his face. His entire mouth glowed bluish-white and the spots trailed down all the way to the floor. She hoped he could not see her, as she could not look away from the many glowing spots.

"Little Sabrina," he whispered in the room. "I see your eyes, so white under this black light. I know you can see how the blood glows under its light. But you ... you are for later. You shall provide my most crucial sustenance."

He then turned and walked to the door, opening it. She held her breath until he closed it behind him.

Sabrina felt more warmth leaking from down below. She knew she had to get away, but she did not try to fight her bonds.

Something slick and wet, not cold, but not quite warm, dripped from the mattress above her onto her face. Sabrina tried to wipe it away with one shoulder, but she couldn't reach.

Another drop splashed her.

She twisted her body and remembered the raw, rough wood at the top of the footboard on her bed where the family dog had gnawed it into splinters. Sabrina slid down and lifted her ankles. She slid her heel along the top of the footboard until she found the rough spot, and started sliding her ankles side to side, the rough wood catching the tape binding her.

When she tired, she stopped. When she felt she could get three or four swipes, she did it again.

In under ten minutes, the tape on her ankles shredded through, and she separated her feet. She swung

174

her feet down to the floor and immediately felt chunks of something wet beneath them.

She looked down. Under the soft glow of the black light, she saw bright spots everywhere. Between her toes it felt like she was walking on dog food spilled from Nebraska's bowl – the dog who had chewed her footboard. He had been a Great Dane that her daddy had said wasn't so great.

She thanked him now.

Thank you, Nebraska.

She sawed the tape on her wrists.

A sound came from outside her door. A slam and a whimper.

More tears came. Sabrina rubbed her taped wrists faster and harder against the jagged footboard.

The tape broke free and her wrists came apart. Sabrina then tore the rest of the clinging tape from her ankles before slowly removing the piece from her mouth.

She moved toward the door and turned the knob, pulling it slowly open and peering out into the living room to see what was happening.

*****

They hit the westbound bridge at 11:15. An accident in midtown Fort Myers had bunged up US-41 southbound and they had to cut through the side streets. Jack did so the moment the traffic slowed. It wasn't out of the question to have police checkpoints during a manhunt, and Jack did not want to get caught in one with Sims in the back.

175

It only slowed them a little. Jack turned to glance at Sims.

"You okay, Sims?" he asked. "I hate to bring this up because I know it's not your fault, but – "

"But you're starting to stink," interrupted Wayne. "Right? He's reeking."

"Yeah."

"I told you," said Sims. "I need food. I feel it. Call it instinctive. Is there any way you can … hey. I know. Turn left on Summerlin."

Jack looked at him in the rear view mirror. "What's on Summerlin?"

"There's a big field on the left side, about half a mile south of College Parkway. Some guy is breeding Alpacas there. At least they were there like a month ago."

"You wanna eat a fucking Alpaca?" asked Wayne.

"Better he eat them than us or someone else," said Jack, easing into the left lane. "Let's just do this so he doesn't fall apart on us."

"Do we even need him anymore?"

"I'm *right* here," said Sims. "My ears still work."

"If we don't find Veselov at Williams' house, yes," said Jack, ignoring Sims' comment but feeling bad about Wayne's lack of tact.

"If I eat I'll be stronger," said Sims. "I know it from the poodle and the rat. My brain works better. I think I can see him wherever he is, like I saw him in that house. All I had to do was close my eyes and think of him earlier," said Sims. "It was right there behind my eyes as clear as day, but I can't do it now."

Jack put his blinker on and made the turn when the green arrow gave him the right-of-way. "I don't see as we have a choice," he said. "We need him to be on his game, and he *did* see Veselov in that house."

"Didn't you get any satisfaction from my freakin' leg?" asked Wayne.

"Not much," said Sims. "Tainted meat."

"I'll taint your meat, dickhead," said Olsen.

"I think I know where he's talking about," Jack said. "Up here by Brantley Road." He turned and smiled at his friend. "How's your leg, by the way?"

"It's throbbing. What kind of house doesn't have antibiotic ointment?"

"You know why Sims gives it to you so bad, right?" asked Jack. "Because you can't fire him and you can't kill him."

"I hate criminals and politicians with nothin' to lose," said Olsen. "Living dead cops, too, I guess."

"Right here," said Jack, eyeing several of the hairy animals in the moonlight. "I see … around eight of them. Maybe more in that little shelter over there."

"Either of you got a knife?" asked Sims.

"I have a pocket knife," said Wayne. "You gonna knife one?"

"Gunfire wouldn't be smart," said Jack. "Look for a rock, too, Sims. Maybe you can stun one before you kill it." He looked at Wayne. "You're not going to be any help. I'll help him tag one. You stay in the car and think of what's next."

"How the hell am I going to explain all the muck inside this damned car?" asked Wayne. A light went on in his eyes and he snapped his fingers. "He's bad enough

177

already, but we don't need anymore blood and stuff on him. Sims, take off your clothes before you eat it."

"I had to check, but apparently the modesty switch has been turned off," said Sims. "I'm so excited about eating, I'll do whatever you want."

"Then you have your orders. Hurry."

Jack and the late Officer Justin Sims got out of the patrol car and approached the fence.

*****

"Wake up!" shouted Veselov, pressing his foot into Officer Williams' stomach. Williams stirred.

The moment he opened his eyes, Veselov swung the arm at him, catching him squarely in the cheekbone. Blood spattered on his face, and he tried to scream beneath the duct tape, but to no avail.

"Oh, this won't do. I must hear you promise to be quiet before I remove the tape. I want to hear what you have to say." The small, severed arm hung limp from his hand.

Williams said something that sounded like "Mmmm mmmmmm!"

"No promise? That is okay."

Veselov reached down with one massive hand and grabbed the SWAT officer's wife, lifting her up over his head. "Perhaps I should throw her through the back door and go and get your daughter."

Williams' head bolted back and forth and his eyes were as round as tiny moons. They kept moving from his wife to the item in Veselov's other hand. The tin man's wife was crying uncontrollably under her makeshift gag.

"No? So you'll be quiet? Very well."

Sergei reached down and tore the tape from his mouth unceremoniously.

The moment the tape was off, Williams took two deep breaths with his eyes closed and said, "Now put my wife on the couch, please. Mr. Veselov, I'm begging you."

"Oh, so it's Mr. Veselov now," said Sergei. "Perhaps you should remember that I am of Krovozhadnost. Your begging is wasted breath."

"Let her go," Williams said again, defeat in his tone that was music to Sergei's ears. "Take me," he said. "Just leave my wife and daughter alone. I did nothing to your family."

Veselov's anger boiled up in an instant. He drew his arm back and flung Kelly Williams through the air toward the rear sliding glass door. She smashed through it, her broken body tumbling all the way to the swimming pool before rolling over the coping and disappearing into the water.

"No!" cried Williams, tears pouring from his eyes. "No ... not my Kelly. Not my son."

"I never said your son was dead," said Veselov. "I have only his arm here." He drew it back and hit Williams so hard he fell unconscious again.

"Damnit," said Veselov. He wanted to torture the SWAT cop, but he wasn't as tough as he had hoped.

He walked out to the back yard and looked around. He turned to the left and right, listening.

Nothing. No alerted neighbors. Sergei moved toward the pool, the water still churning from the officer's wife's entry.

"The team from Mother Russia would have beat you in the diving competition," he said. "Very big splash."

With that, Sergei dropped Darrin Williams' arm and jumped into the water, sinking to the bottom. His eyes open, he saw the dark figure on the bottom of the pool, and bent down to retrieve her.

He lifted her and placed her body on the edge of the pool. Her neck was clearly broken.

She would not be warm for very much longer. He crawled out of the pool and picked her up. He carried her inside and lay her three feet in front of the cop. He casually walked back outside to the pool deck and retrieved the boy's limb.

With a few taps on the shoulder with the extremity, Williams was again awake and horrified. He said nothing. He stared at his dead wife, her head turned in an unnatural position.

"Yes, she is dead. Now you will watch as I gain strength from her, just as I did your boy."

He threw the arm to the dining table, and it landed in a centerpiece basket in the middle. Veselov smiled at the soon-to-be-dead officer. "Two points," he said.

Williams closed his eyes.

"If you try to do that while I eat your wife," said Sergei, with a smile, "I will cut off your eyelids."

*****

Jack followed Sims into the field. The dead cop removed his clothing fifteen feet or so inside the fence so no drivers passing by on Summerlin would spot the nude

180

man. Even if they did, the police car might convince them that they were already taking care of it.

After piling the clothes Wayne had given him neatly in the grass, Sims seemed to have found a burst of energy, simply by just being close to his potential food source. Even with his strange gait and reattached leg, Sims moved swiftly across the five-acre pasture, chewed short by the grazing animals. He cut left and cut right, the small pocket knife in his hands, and sure enough, he quickly found success, driving a smaller, white Alpaca into the corner of the corral.

Jack moved toward them, ready to block off the only escape path for the animal. The animal made a humming-clicking sound as it moved toward Sims, and as the cop took two steps toward him, it tried to dart toward Jack.

By the time it saw Jack there and turned back, Sims had hooked an arm around it and plunged the knife into the creature's neck, drawing it along until its knees buckled.

Sims fell atop it and flipped it over to find the underbelly. With a single glance up at Jack, he again focused on the still convulsing animal.

It took Sims twenty-five minutes. The more he consumed the more energy he seemed to have, and the faster he ate the animal, his hands pulling apart the fleece and burrowing in.

Jack turned away and silently hoped there was a water hose inside the shelter.

There weren't enough napkins in all the McDonald's in the world to clean up the mess that was Justin Sims.

181

*****

Sabrina had run to her bed, but she could not get in it. The stuff dripping down from above had now soaked her mattress, and she nearly slipped in the chunks on the floor. She cried, her entire body shaking, but she knew she had to be quiet, so very quiet.

When she had opened the door and peeked out, she couldn't see the people, but she heard her daddy's voice and another man who talked funny. The same man who had been in her room.

She had opened the door only a crack, but it was enough. She saw the man step into her view. He was holding something that looked like part of a big doll. It was an arm with a hand.

A moment later, she saw her mommy flying through the air, and she flew right through the sliding glass door like the little bird had done last month. It got a broken neck and died.

She had closed the door then, as slowly and quietly as she could, like when she got up in the middle of the night and followed the refrigerator light to get water.

Now she stood by the window and pulled the blind string up as slowly as she could. It made a little sound, but she hardly heard it over her own breathing.

A thump in the other room. Sabrina held her breath, her hands freezing like a statue.

The little brunette girl waited, feeling every pound of her heart. After what she counted as a hundred of her own heartbeats, she pulled some more.

Now it was high enough. She reached up and found the latch and spun it. Sabrina hooked her little fingers beneath the ledge of the window and pulled.

And pulled.

And pulled. She strained, her fingers hurting, her arms shaking, until it broke free and slid upward fast. She almost lost her balance and fell backward, but she was lucky her shoes were off because her bare foot did not make a sound.

Sabrina was glad she thought of her shoes. She tiptoed to her closet and got her tennies on. They were Hello Kitty tennies and they were almost brand new, so she knew they would help her run like the wind.

She pulled and pressed on the Velcro straps and stood. Moving to the window, she raised her leg to step through it and into the darkness beyond.

She thought, *Be brave, Sabrina.* As she put her left leg out, she lost her balance for a moment and hit something that tore. It wasn't loud, so she didn't worry about the man in the other room hearing it, but then she remembered.

She had forgotten about the screen! Mommy and Daddy would be so mad!

Something splashed in the swimming pool. She did not know what it was, but it was where mommy had flown through the air.

Should she go there? Push through the screen and run to the back of the house? Yes. Yes, it was exactly what she would do, and if the man saw them, she and mommy would run. Her mommy would keep her safe.

183

She threw her foot up again and pushed through the hole. It tore a little and then the whole thing popped out and fell to the ground.

She held her breath again.

Nothing. She climbed through. Once her feet were on the ground, she turned left and ran toward the back of the house.

Something – she wasn't sure what – told her to slow down before she got to the corner of the house. The entire pool area was enclosed in a giant screened cage. She reached it and leaned around the corner, watching.

The man was there. The doll arm was on the ground and he was in the pool. Sabrina watched as he lifted something from the water.

She saw what it was. Her mommy, her head hanging limp like the bird. It was just like the bird.

The bird had been dead. That meant mommy was dead.

Sabrina turned and ran along the side of the house as fast as she could, trying to beat the wailing cry bubbling up from inside of her that she knew she would not be able to stop.

She knew she should run, but instead she stopped just past her window and dropped down to her bottom against the house. She needed to cry for a while. She was already out of breath and had no idea where to run.

Her sobs would not stop shaking her body, and the more she cried, the more she felt like crying.

Just a few minutes rest. Then she would run to her friend's house, just down at the end of the street.

At that moment she remembered. Her new bicycle was in the front yard.

*****

Veselov used a knife from the kitchen to cut Kelly Williams open. Her blood ran over the hardwood floor as he used the knife to cut chunks of her away and devour them.

He looked up at Williams and said, "I never had a taste for human flesh before, and I never enjoyed rare meat. Now I find that both are very good."

Williams had his face turned away. Veselov did not like that.

"Look!" he shouted. "You watch! You killed me, so you will watch as I kill everyone you care about. You will be last for you will –"

A high pitched wailing sound interrupted his words. He suddenly jerked upward, straightening up until he stood on his knees. "What the hell?" he said. Tiny red lights had just flickered by outside the window facing the side of the house. The thin blind was closed, but the reflection was as clear as day.

Veselov got to his feet. "Get up!" he shouted at Williams. "Now!"

"I can't!" shouted Williams. "My feet! What's wrong? What are you doing?"

Veselov reached down and used the knife to slice through the duct tape. "Try anything and I will kill you even more slowly and painfully. Get up!"

Williams obeyed his command. He bent down and snatched the half-eaten carcass of Kelly Williams from the floor and threw her over his shoulder. With his other large hand, he grabbed Williams, who was around 5'-10"

185

tall, by the neck and shook him. "What kind of car do you have?"

"Wh-what?" stammered Williams.

"The car! What kind!" shouted the Russian.

"A 2013 Malibu!" said Williams.

"Get your keys and get to the garage now!"

"They're in the kitchen," he sobbed, turning to his right and trying to avoid the bloody chunks on the floor and averting his eyes from his son's severed arm.

Sergei stayed right on him, and he grabbed the arm from the basket, slapped Williams in the back of the head with it before dropping it on the floor.

Williams stopped and doubled over, emptying the contents of his stomach on the kitchen tiles.

"Hurry!" shouted Veselov, pushing him further into the kitchen. Williams stumbled forward and caught himself against the counter. He reached up and grabbed the keys from a hook next to the refrigerator.

"Go!"

Williams moved slowly. "Please, spare the rest of us. I was doing my job," he pleaded.

"I am doing now what I do," said Sergei. "Open the trunk."

The Chevrolet had been backed into the garage, so there was room to get to the trunk. Williams stared at the car, then at Veselov. "Why?"

"Because it is where you will stay until I get your daughter."

"What do you mean?" said Williams, turning.

"I mean she is running away now. In!"

"Run, Sabrina!" shouted Williams, charging toward the closed garage door. "If you can hear me, run and don't stop!"

Sergei released the body of the officer's wife, allowing it to crumple to the concrete garage floor before charging toward Williams, whose wrists were still bound together. Sergei bear hugged him from behind and dragged the distraught officer backward before pushing him against the car and hammering an elbow into his head.

The SWAT officer fell unconscious and collapsed into the Malibu's trunk like a sack of laundry. Sergei then retrieved the ravaged, dripping body of Kelly Williams from the floor and deposited the corpse on top of the cop.

He slammed the trunk lid closed and ran back into the house. He did not stop until he reached the little girl's room to confirm what he suspected had happened. The boy was where he had left him, but the blind was up and the window was open.

The little girl named Sabrina was gone.

*****

Sabrina had trouble opening the fence to get from the side yard into the front. The string that hung down was just out of her reach, but on the third jump, she caught it between her thumb and her pointing finger and the latch clicked up.

The seven-year-old reached her bicycle in the front yard and then remembered that she had chained it to the

187

oak tree. She knew the combination was 4-3-6-0, so all she had to do was roll the wheels around and pull it apart.

Her hands shook like the little hamster she used to have did when she picked it up. The moon kept drifting behind clouds, but she could still see the numbers, so she tried to focus. That's what her daddy told her to do when she was learning to tie her shoes.

Focus, Sabrina, she thought to herself as the last number rolled into place.

She pulled the lock apart and dropped the chain.

"Run, Sabrina!" It was all she heard that she could understand, but it was her daddy's voice. Then something slammed in the garage. She looked at the house, saw nobody coming out the front door, and she scrambled onto her bicycle and pushed with her feet until she reached the sidewalk. Pushing her feet over the curb, she rode into the street without noticing the car coming until she was right in front of it.

It was moving fast. She closed her eyes and heard tires screeching on the pavement.

*****

The girl came out of nowhere.

"Watch out!" shouted Wayne, as Jack just spotted her and cranked the wheel hard to the right to avoid hitting the child on the bicycle. The car hit the low curb hard, bouncing into the air and across the lawn of a house.

Jack saw the tree as it fast approached his windshield. A moment later his body slammed forward and two dust-filled explosions filled his ears. Stunned,

188

he felt as though he had been a rock in the leather pocket of a slingshot that had just been fired into a wall.

He didn't know how long he sat there. Time seemed to have stopped. When Jack became aware again, Officer Sims stood outside his door. He pulled on the door handle a few times as Jack stared, trying to organize a thought. The deflated airbags lay limp over the dashboard, as Jack looked through the shattered front windshield to see crumpled metal. It was the police cruiser's hood, poking through to the interior of the car.

"Jack, you okay, man?" asked Wayne.

He turned to see Wayne, his nose disjointed sideways, staring at him. Blood ran down his mouth and chin.

"What the hell? Did we hit her?" asked Jack.

"I didn't see, man. I think we missed her. You turned that wheel and it was all a blur from there. I think my nose is broken."

Suddenly the side window of the police cruiser blew in, and hundreds of crystalline squares landed in Jack's lap.

"This is the house!" said Sims. He reached down again and brushed the remainder of the side window away, grabbing the top of the door frame with both hands.

"I'll crawl out the –"

Before Jack could finish, Sims ripped the entire door off the car and heaved it across the lawn as though it weighed nothing. "Now get the fuck out of there! We have to get Veselov!"

"Jesus, Sims!" shouted Wayne.

"I didn't wreck the car! Hurry!" he shouted.

189

Jack reached down to disconnect his seatbelt when a sound came from across the lawn. It was the garage door.

It was lifting.

Sims reached down and snatched Jack's gun from his side holster. He turned and ran toward the garage, the door now fully up.

The car's engine revved and it shot out of the garage like a bullet.

Sims, still ever the cop, took a firing stance and blew out the passenger side window. From where he sat in the car, Jack could see who was at the wheel.

It was Sergei Veselov. Jack pushed the seatbelt release and it came open and he crawled out.

"I'm comin' behind you," said Wayne, and Jack stopped and turned to help him when another report of a gun blasted away the stillness of the night, followed by the sound of more shattering safety glass.

Jack spun around to follow the car as it burned rubber down the street and became nothing more than taillights.

He held out his arm. "We're in over our heads, Wayne. We need to call in the cavalry."

*****

CHAPTER EIGHT

It was not late, but Hannah Maruska couldn't sleep. She thought about Jack Hunger, the man she had long loved in her heart, but who had lost all confidence in both himself and in the opposite sex.

Hannah knew what that was like. When she and her brother had come to America from the Czech Republic, she had met a boy from her country shortly thereafter. It was comfortable because they both spoke the same language and both knew pretty good English, too. He often made playful advances toward her, and she playfully declined.

She had believed that would be the last word. Back and forth. He tried, she said no, they both laughed.

One day there was no laughing. He had wanted her and she had rejected him. He had beaten her to the point where she felt as though she would die if one more blow landed.

He left then, and she had not seen him since. Her brother, who never knew the entire story, said he had moved to North Dakota to work in the oil shale industry.

She got out of bed and made her decision. She reached for the phone and held it in her hands, staring at the clock. It was just past midnight.

She smiled. That meant it was tomorrow. She dialed Jack's cell phone.

*****

When the phone in his pocket rang, Jack almost didn't know what it was. He looked down, saw the light through his pants pocket, and reached in.

Wayne was out of the car now, leaning against it, trying to use both of his palms flat against his nose to reset it. It wasn't going well, at least in Jack's eyes.

He did not recognize the number. "Hello?" he said.

"Jack? It's Hannah."

Jack's mind spun. He looked at his watch. It was after midnight. Almost 12:30.

"Hannah, hi," he said, awkwardly. "What's wrong? Are you alright?"

"I'm fine, Jack. I'm fine. I just … I wanted to … I don't know."

"Why did you call my cell?"

"I tried your home but you did not answer," she explained.

"Nah, I know it's late, but I'm still at the office. Probably won't be home for three or four hours yet. It's that case with the Russian. It's more complex than I thought."

192

"I don't want to bother you then, Jack. I just wanted to tell you something."

Sims was inside the house and Wayne had limped in after him. Jack stared at the open garage door and looked at the phone in his hand. "What's that, Hannah? I'm sorry if I seem distracted. It's nice to hear from you."

"It's nice to talk to you, but I will just tell you that you may have a surprise waiting when you get home."

"What do you mean?"

"I have the key," she said. "Good bye, Jack."

The phone disconnected and Jack slid it back into his pocket.

He couldn't for the life of him figure out what she was talking about.

*****

Before Veselov hit the end of the street he spotted the girl on her bicycle riding unsteadily toward a house on the corner of the street. He saw her look back, and he hit the gas hard.

The Malibu did not respond as some of the older models still on the streets in Moscow would have, but it charged forward and he slammed on the brakes as she rolled onto the grass of the corner house and dropped the bicycle.

He threw the door open and ran full speed. Her scream was unexpected – he wasn't certain why – and piercing.

She had stopped to stare at him before she screamed. He scooped her up and turned in two steps, and in three giant leaps more, he was back at the car, throwing her inside head first.

She hit the opposite door and crumpled to the floorboard. He wasn't done with this family yet, but one thing was certain: He needed to lay low somewhere for a few hours.

Sergei saw people coming out of the houses around him and floored the accelerator. He turned right at the end of the street and headed east. He would search for a home with a for sale sign in the yard or perhaps some tall grass, saying nobody was residing there at the moment.

He found several within a couple of blocks, but he needed to put more distance between him and the carnage he had left behind.

The entire city would be worse than the scene in that single house in Lehigh Acres before long.

*****

"He's picked clean," said Sims, standing beside the bunk bed.

Jack walked into the bedroom behind Wayne and stared for only a moment before realizing that what was in the top bunk was the remains of a young boy.   In the living room they'd found multiple bullet holes in the wall and other far more disturbing evidence of violence unlike any Jack had ever experienced before.

"This *is* Williams' house, right?" asked Jack. Just because there were dead people and signs of a struggle did not mean Veselov had reached his final destination. Surely he was capable of making a mistake.

194

"We're at the right place," said Wayne, still holding his nose, his voice nasally. "Fuck. Get away from him, Sims."

"I don't know Derek Williams very well," said Jack, "but I know he has two kids. That must've been his girl on the bicycle."

Sims turned. "She's next if he caught her. We need to get to him. I can't believe we were that close."

"Again, *Mr. Alpaca*," remarked Wayne. "Next time it's no poodles and no alpacas. We go where we say, when we say it. I think you'll admit we'd have had him if not for your meal stop."

"Yeah, and how would I have fought him? Look at this." He raised his left arm. "I noticed it in the car."

Wayne and Jack leaned in to see. "What the hell?" asked Jack. The area of skin that was severed appeared to be scabbing over. He looked at Sims. "You're healing?"

Sims shrugged. "I don't know. I've never been dead and dismembered before. That's what it looks like to me."

"Well, either we're getting used to him or he doesn't smell as bad as earlier," said Wayne. "What do you mean how would you have fought him?"

"I'm stronger with food," said Sims. "Plus it's reattaching my limbs. With enough food, I may be able to overpower and kill him."

"How can he die?" asked Jack. "Do you know?"

If it were possible, Sims again looked nervous. He walked toward the bedroom door before stopping and turning around. "Sheriff, you see how I took that car door off with my hands?"

Wayne nodded.

"I'll do that with his head. I know I can. I've got a ton of rage boiling up inside of me because that big, dead fuck took me from my family and left my daughter and my child-to-be without a father, and he left my wife a widow. Williams only killed him, and I doubt he cares about his family very much if at all."

"So is this your ... dying wish? To be the one to kill him?" asked Wayne.

"After the fact, but yes sir," said Sims.

Jack interjected. "Okay, so can you do that thing with your ... I don't know ... that projection thing? Can you see him?"

Sims walked out of the child's room and into the living room. There were chunks of gore all over the floor, and one of the boy's arms lay beneath the dining table. Jack turned his face away. "We need to call this in."

"I have a funny feeling the Cape cops will be here in no time."

"I'm going to look for a car," said Jack, leaving the room. "Sims, see if you can get a location on Veselov. Wayne, sit the hell down. How's your nose?"

"Can't breathe through it, but I have a mouth, so no loss. My modeling days are over."

"The fans of Playgirl will forever be in mourning," said Jack. "Sims, find him. Wayne, sit." He left the room.

*****

Though he was being drawn to the south, Veselov did not know why. He instead guided the Malibu west, then as a compromise to his instinct, he drove three miles before turning west, into south Cape Coral. He saw SW 25th Street and made the turn.

There were few homes on that particular roadway. He was not certain why, but he guessed it was because it backed up to the busy main road, and the noise likely chased away potential builders or buyers. Sergei glanced to his right and saw that a canal also ran behind the house, between the busy street and the property line.

Sergei liked the traffic noise; it meant that the residents here were probably used to tuning noise out. He liked the canal because if anything went wrong, he could jump in and sink to the bottom. He did not breathe, so it would be easy to just walk away, unseen beneath the still, dark waters.

The sign he saw on the right was unexpected and perfect. It read Select Realty Associates. Agent Linda Mihalovich was the listing agent, and the rider on top said "SPEC HOME."

Even Sergei knew that meant it had been built to sell. All of the windows were dark, and there were no personal effects out front; no flower pots, no welcome mat.

The lot beside it was empty. Sergei pulled the Chevy onto the dead grass and drove until he was ten yards off the street.

The girl was out, but he could not take the chance she would remain so. He picked her up and got out as she stirred in his arms.

197

Using the key remote, he opened the trunk. He leaned forward to lower the child into the trunk. He rested her atop her mother's corpse as he felt cold steel strike the side of his head.

"Aaaaaahhh!" shouted Williams, rising from the trunk and drawing back the tire iron again, now on his knees behind his wife's body, double gripping it and swinging hard.

Veselov was not hurt, but the iron had hit him in the temple, and his eye filled with blackness, temporarily blinding him. He thrust his hands out in front of him and one of them caught the bar in mid swing.

Sergei took it and turned the pry end toward his unseen attacker. He jammed it forward and heard the sound of a man in agony.

Blinking away the blackness, Sergei staggered away from the trunk for a moment. He used his filthy sleeves to again try to clear his vision, and it slowly returned.

He looked over at the car.

Williams lay on his back, his eyes closed. The tire iron protruded from the right side of chest, and through his white undershirt, Sergei could see a spot of blood growing larger and larger.

Warm blood. Fresh blood.

Empowering blood.

He unceremoniously threw Williams' dead body forward and lowered the trunk, pressing it softly until it latched. He turned and scanned the street and the neighborhood.

Nobody. He went to unlock the house. He would rest here, but only until he finished with the Williams family. He had one more stop to make tonight – the most important of all, perhaps – before returning to Krovozhadnost.

He knew that when he returned to his mafia family, he would be invincible; the most powerful member there had ever been. Nobody would challenge him. He would do as he wished.

As he approached the rear screen enclosure, he pressed the button on the door handle and it pulled open. He moved to the rear sliding glass door and saw that indeed, the home was unfurnished. He lifted up on the sliding door and popped the lock.

He was in. The Russian returned to the vehicle to get his food. He wished Williams had not tried to be a hero. Now he was dead and he had deprived Sergei of torturing him properly.

He would take his pleasure instead by substituting Derek Williams' daughter for him.

*****

Hannah's mother had died of cervical cancer when she was just fifteen years old. Three years later, after waiting for all of their visas and documentation to be in order, she, her brother and their father came to America. It was always Hugo Maruska's dream to live in the land of the free and the home of the brave, and he vowed his children would know such a place.

Even if his wife had not lived to do it with them.

Of course he had difficulty finding well-paying employment, though he was an excellent leatherworker, and did find work in a local upholsterer's shop. It was hard work and he came home tired. He was asleep as

Hannah went to the kitchen to gather some supplies. She intended to make Jack breakfast. She would get everything ready and make it as soon as he came in the door.

Of course she knew what Jack had at his place; she had cleaned it since shortly after his ex-girlfriend, Debra, had turned in her notice.

She knew that he was short on eggs, so she brought four. She had some small potatoes, so she brought them as well to make him some hash browns. He had sausage she could thaw from the freezer.

Wouldn't he be surprised when he came in to the smell of a nice breakfast. She knew he had not eaten; Jack wasn't the type the stop in the middle of his work for his own benefit. It was always about the job for him.

Hannah smiled at the thought of him. She hoped he would kiss her. She had come so close to his mouth when she had kissed him good-bye that she felt a tingle down there. Instinctive, and unmistakable.

Checking on her father once more, Hannah tiptoed out of the house and got in her old Nissan Sentra and set out to Jack Hunger's house.

*****

"We need to steal a car," said Olsen.

"You've lost your mind," said Jack.

"Whatever you're going to do, you need to … hey. Who's car is that?" Sims asked.

"Which one?"

"I see it," said Olsen, through clogged nostrils. He pointed. "That one there. In the street by the field."

200

Jack checked the street behind them, saw no police cars ripping toward them and hurried to the car. Wayne limped behind.

Jack reached the old Toyota first and peered through the window. Before Wayne even reached the car, Jack recoiled and bent over, supporting himself with his hands on his knees. "Shit. This is so far out of hand we're fucked."

In the back seat of the car, a woman's body lay shredded. Any part of her that could be eaten was gnawed down to the bone. Her head and torso lay on the seat and her ravaged legs splayed into the passenger side floorboard.

Jack pulled the driver's door open and leaned in. He looked back at Wayne. "He left the keys."

"I ain't gettin' in that thing," said Wayne.

"Yes, you are," Jack ordered. "Both of you get the hell in the car now. We need to get off this street and we need to do it fast. You saw the bullet holes in the wall in there, and this ain't exactly inner city Chicago. Calls have been made and they've probably already tried to stir Williams and can't reach him."

"Shit, that's right," said Wayne. "The Cape uses our county SWAT, and if they know the call is near his house, they'll dispatch him."

Jack got in the driver's seat and turned the key. The engine fired, and he leaned over and opened the glove compartment. He pulled out a registration card and read it. "Tina Oakes. She was twenty-four years old."

He looked at the fuel gauge and saw it was topped off. Ever the detective, he looked between the seats and found a bloodstained receipt. He picked it up.

ERIC A. SHELMAN

"He got this car at the gas station. She filled up there just a little while ago. That's where his car is, and they have surveillance. It won't be long before they have a BOLO out for this car."

"Go then," said Wayne. "Sims, close your goddamned eyes and try to see that bastard. No more poodles or Alpacas."

"I might be interested to see if there's enough of her left then," he said sheepishly. "If I need more strength, you're going to have to deal with it."

Wayne reached down and took his gun from its holster. He held it to Sims' neck. "That's not going to happen," he said. "And just one attempt at biting me will result in more of your inky black shit spraying that window. Now close your eyes and look for the Russian."

Jack drove, hoping Sims would tell him which direction to turn.

*****

Sergei knew the woman was a lost cause. It was disappointing, because she would have provided him much needed strength if only she were fresh.

Williams himself was still warm. In fact, on second inspection, Sergei had found a slight heartbeat. He dared not remove the tire iron, or his lifeblood would leak out and he would die.

Sergei preferred his meat with circulation. A new discovery.

He had dropped two rolls of duct tape into the trunk, and he used them to bind the girl again. She was still out or she was pretending; it did not matter. She would be

202

gone before he attempted his final mission before returning to Krovozhadnost. Wouldn't they be surprised.

And frightened. They would be rightfully afraid. Nobody would challenge the invincible Sergei Veselov.

There was power on in the house, but no overhead lights. A streetlight shone through the front window and Sergei could see well enough by that. He went into the kitchen and saw the clock glowing on the microwave. It was not flashing, and it read 1:40.

Plenty of darkness left to accomplish what he needed. He went to Williams and bent over to lift his body. Not a small man, and Veselov did not even feel the dead weight as he hoisted him into his arms and carried him into the faint light of the living room.

The blinds were cheap, plastic mini-blinds. There were no curtains. The carpeting was dark brown and cheap, the padding beneath worn and flattened.

As Veselov put Williams down on the floor, his eyes fluttered open. He stared straight at Sergei for a few seconds, then his blank expression turned to horror.

He turned his face toward his daughter, unconscious against the opposite wall.

"You want I should wake her?" he asked. "Before I eat you?"

"No ... pl –"

His words were cut short when he winced and squeezed his eyes closed.

"Stay awake," said Sergei. He lifted Williams' arm and he brought it up to his mouth. He stretched open his jaws and took a huge bite out of his forearm, his front teeth scraping against the bone.

Williams screamed, then fell silent.

203

"Fuck it," said Veselov. He reached up and yanked the embedded tire iron from Williams' chest and drew back his arm. He smashed it into the side of the cop's head. Once, twice, three and four times. The skull cracked open, but Sergei kept at it, and when it was shattered enough, he leaned forward and spread the cracked skull apart.

He feasted until he heard a little girl's dull scream behind him, muffled by duct tape.

Power surged through his veins. He held the bloody crowbar in the air and bent it into the shape of a "U."

He no longer heard the girl's screams.

He closed his eyes and a room swam into view.

Sergei Veselov knew where he needed to go.

*****

"I can't do it!"

"Then you're useless to us," said Wayne.

"I need to feed on her."

Jack turned from the front seat. He was parked on SW 17th Avenue, a street that mostly consisted of businesses. It was late enough in Cape Coral that should a police car come by now, they would be interested in the men sitting in the Toyota, particularly if Veselov's other vehicle had been found at the gas station.

No telling what he'd left inside that one.

Jack looked at Sims, then at Wayne. "I don't know if he was in a hurry or not, but it looks like there's more … fuck." He choked down something that threatened to come up his throat and continued, glancing down at the remains beside him. "Looks like there's more meat on her."

Just saying the words disgusted Jack.

"I said no!" Wayne protested. "There's no way I'm keepin' my job after this is over, Jack. I've already fucked that possibility with what I've let happen so far tonight. If we're not on some surveillance video somewhere I'd be shocked."

"Then we have to do what we can to save the lives of anyone else who might be at risk."

"He won't stop," said Sims. "If you two weren't here right now, I don't know if I'd be able to stop myself." He pointed at the end of the street. "I'd go right in that house there and I'd go to the bedroom and kill whoever was in that bed, and I'd eat them. The feeling is that strong. And I was a good guy."

"She's already dead, Wayne," said Jack.

"You swear it will be enough?" asked Wayne.

Sims nodded, but with the rebar in his neck, his shoulders had to participate too. "I can't promise anything after, but it will help me find him."

Jack fired the engine and pulled the Toyota into the dark parking lot of an insurance adjustment company. He parked the car, turned off the key and got out.

Wayne opened the back door and got out as well.

"You need to call your wife?" asked Jack.

"I'm almost afraid to."

"Why?"

"For fear it'll be the last time I talk to her."

"Really?"

Wayne looked at Jack. "Hunger, this is occult shit. Demonic shit. Dead people coming back to life.

Dismembered people helping us. Maybe we're not supposed to make it through this."

"If I stop to think about any of it too long, I'm going to check myself into a mental institution," said Jack. "I need to have some time to sit down and just pore over everything that's gone on."

Wayne shook his head. "If I live through this I might start going to church again."

Jack checked his watch. "Liquor sales just cut off."

"Cops'll be out in force now, lookin' for drunks."

"We don't need to get caught in a checkpoint."

Sirens broke the night, and through the buildings they saw six Cape Coral Police Department cars jamming south.

"Jig's up," said Wayne.

"Once they see that kid's arm and whosoever remains those were splattered on the floor of the living room, they're going to tie it to what happened to Kathryn Hightower," said Jack.

"No way they can't. Too brutal and out of the ordinary for around here," said Wayne.

"The black stuff," said Jack. "Like ink."

Wayne held up his fingers. They were all stained black, as were Jack's. "It's gotta be some kind of ink," he said.

"Sims said something in your garage," said Jack. "About another place he needs to go after he kills Veselov."

"I didn't hear it."

"Every time I've asked him about it, he avoids the question. I see some kind of lie in his eyes, but with him

206

in that condition, I can't tell. He's not exactly the typical interviewee."

"Is he done yet?" asked Wayne. "And can we move her to the trunk? Too risky having her in the cab, not to mention too fucking disgusting."

*****

They found two old moving blankets in the trunk of the car and pulled them out. After pulling the woman's carcass from the passenger side of the car, they rested it atop one of the blankets and wrapped all of the sides over her.

Jack was almost sickened again at how light the body was to carry; she had been nearly completely consumed by Veselov and Sims.

"Okay," said Sims afterward. "I saw him. I wasn't able to focus long enough to get an address."

"What about mail, like last time?" asked Wayne.

"There's no furniture in the house," said Sims. "Like it's vacant. There's nothing in there except him, Williams and the girl."

"She's still alive?" asked Jack.

"I think so," said Sims. "She might be asleep. I guess she could be dead."

"Appreciate the nonchalant attitude," said Wayne.

"It is what it is," said Sims.

"Go back," said Jack. "We need an address. Can you move around like before?"

"Yes, I'm pretty sure. I got a weird feeling, though."

"Like what?"

"I don't know exactly. Like he … felt me."

"Is this a problem?" asked Wayne.

"I don't know if he can do anything about it, or if I'm even right, so the answer is, I don't know."

"What was he doing when you were there?" asked Jack.

"Working on Officer Williams," said Sims. "Gotta admit, I was kind of jealous."

"I'll fucking shoot you. One more remark like that."

"Wayne," said Jack. "We don't have the luxury, plus it doesn't do anything to him."

"So what do we do when this is over? How do we put you to rest, Sims?"

Sims didn't answer.

Jack walked toward him. "What is it?"

"I don't know," said Sims.

"I guess that answers the question about whether the dead can lie," said Jack.

"Was that *ever* a question?' asked Sims.

"Not anymore," said Jack. "I need to know."

"I feel a need to protect something. It feels connected to my existence, but I'm not sure what it is.

"You need to figure it out," said Jack.

Sims shook his head. "Veselov is more urgent. If he's the same as me, his focus will change when he's done with Williams. Whatever that other thing is, and wherever it is, I have a feeling he'll be drawn there, too, and he can't do that. If he does he'll be invincible."

"If you get there, will you be invincible?"

"Depends. I don't know what's there yet."

"You're talking in circles."

"I don't know what it is!" he shouted, black inky spittle flying from his lips.

Jack shielded his face with an open hand, then wiped his face on his forearm sleeve. "Stop spitting that shit in my face!"

"Sorry. Never had this particular problem before," said Sims.

Jack walked to the rear of the car and took the second folded moving blanket, carrying it to the passenger side of the car. He spread it open, folded it in half again, and lay it over the passenger side seat, letting it drape down over the floorboard. He looked over the car at Wayne. "I'll drive again, you sit here."

Wayne walked around. "Looks clean enough." He got in and closed the door.

"Go back, Sims. To the house Veselov's in. Find him."

Sims got in the car and sat in the center of the back seat. "Okay. Here goes nothing."

*****

Hannah pulled her car off to the side of the building and parked. She wanted to completely surprise Jack when he came home.

She had also brought something special to wear. This would be the time for them. Hannah felt the time was perfect. Jack Hunger was over Debra.

She carried her two bags up the steps and put the key in the lock. She opened the door and went inside.

Turning on the light as she entered, she closed and locked the door behind her and put the bags on the kitchen counter.

She walked over to the stereo and sorted through the vinyl albums Jack had in an old peach crate.

This time she chose Aerosmith's Toys In The Attic record, and started with the B side.

The strains of Sweet Emotion drifted across the room as she opened the freezer and removed the sausage. She carried them to the sink and filled it with water, leaving the package to float there and thaw.

From the refrigerator, she removed some green onions and took them from the bag. She would chop them to put in the eggs. There was plenty of cheese, too. Cheddar, his favorite.

Hannah's mind drifted for a moment, her eyes falling to papers stacked beside the telephone. She walked to them and picked up the entire stack. They had not been there when she had cleaned, so her instinct was to put them away, perhaps in Jack's small office.

Turning them over, she stared, unsure what she was seeing there. It took only another second before she realized what it was.

Photographs from the crime scene in Lehigh Acres. The Russian they called Veselov.

She turned one more photograph over and saw the sightless eyes of a man, staring from a severed head lying upward in the dirt.

Hannah suppressed a scream and dropped the pictures. She fell back against the counter, leaning there for a long time, trying to force her heartbeat to return to normal speed.

She breathed deeply and turned her head away, gathering up all of the horrific photographs and stacking them again. She made sure that on top and bottom, the photographs faced inward, and took them into Jack's office.

She looked around. An old briefcase sat under the desk, leaning against one of the legs. Hannah slid it out, undid the flap, and tucked the photographs inside, returning it to where she'd found it.

There.

Thoughts of the horror a man like Jack Hunger might see in his daily work made her heart long to bring him feelings of love and life, rather than bad people and death.

His breakfast and their time together would be a start. She removed the bottle of Champagne she had brought from home. Her father had purchased it to celebrate a promotion that he had expected but that had not come to fruition.

Jack would need it after his day.

*****

CHAPTER NINE

Veselov had stripped Williams' body bare and lay him spread eagle in the center of the living room. He consumed him from the bottom to the top.

With his newfound power and strength, he found it easier to tear a limb from the body as he wanted to eat it. Sergei found he had no desire to use the bathroom and no need or want to drink anything but the blood that slid down his eager throat with the fresh, raw meat.

Sergei wondered if the souls of the men and women he had eaten were what provided him the extraordinary strength and mental capability.

It felt right. The trunk and torso were not as easy to consume; this was a large piece, but the most satisfying. He realized that nothing tasted as sweet as the brain, which he had instinctively eaten first, but all of it was good.

As he was eating the brain, however, he saw the place again; his final destination before leaving this place forever and rejoining his Krovozhadnost.

The child had awakened at least twice, but upon seeing the feast in which Sergei had been engaged, had passed out again. Sergei imagined he could smell her now; his senses were extraordinary. He reached down and snapped a rib free of the body, tearing the sinew and ripping the piece out.

He stood and walked to the front window. It was quiet out. This was a good place to stay.

Suddenly he felt a presence behind him and spun around.

Sergei stared. The man stood there behind him, bloody and strangely familiar. He was not quite solid, as though just a vision rather than a real ... he stepped forward and the man took two steps backward, the expression on his face frightened, but also confused.

Kind of how Sergei felt at the moment. He stared at the face. He knew it. "You are the tin man I killed in the house," he said. "I fucking ripped you to pieces." He pointed at his right leg. "Except for that. I did not have time to take that off."

The vision looked shocked for a moment, staring back at him. Sergei shot his arm out to grab the man, and his hand closed on nothing.

He is drawn to me as I was drawn to my killer. Somehow the same thing has happened to him.

But he was in pieces! Sergei stared at the man standing in front of him. Someone had put him back together, or he would not be like this.

"Who is helping you?" asked Veselov. "How did you become one piece again?"

The man then turned and walked to the front door and Sergei followed. He saw duct tape on some of his

213

joints, and others appeared to be covered with crusty, purplish skin.

Scabs? Was that possible? Would it be so for him? Perhaps he was healing inside even now, as he swallowed the warm flesh of Williams.

Perhaps that was why he was drawn so strongly to his killer; it would be the final healing he needed.

What is he doing? thought Sergei.

The cop reached the door and moved through it, but Sergei could not do the same. He could when he visited Williams' house earlier that evening, in his mind. During that ethereal journey, he could float and move and most importantly, he could *see*.

This was how the tin man and whoever was helping him planned to find him.

Sergei felt pure rage bubble up inside of him. He charged back to where Williams lay and reached down, picking up his entire corpse. He held the body high over his head, one hand gripping it beneath the arm and the other holding on to the leg.

He spread his arms apart and ripped the dead cop's body in two pieces, holding both high above his head.

The familiar apparition came back in through the front wall and stopped abruptly, staring at Sergei and the two pieces of the man he had held. Sergei dropped Williams' body, and it hit the carpet with a wet, squishing impact.

As mysteriously as he had appeared, the tin man was gone.

Sergei looked down at the SWAT officer's body and then looked at the girl. She would stay alive until the very last moment. She would provide the sustenance he needed to ensure his immortality.

*****

"He saw me!" said Sims, appearing very unnerved. "He talked to me. I wanted to kill him right there, but I knew I couldn't. He tried to grab me!"

Jack pulled the car over and put it in park. "What happened?" he asked.

"His hand went through me. I wasn't there, so ... but he saw me that clearly."

"Why didn't he see you before?" asked Wayne.

"Maybe because I wasn't – I don't know – *as* there."

"What do you mean?" asked Jack.

"You know, since I fed on that girl. This was much easier. The minute I closed my eyes I saw him in that living room. I felt like I was there, physically."

"Did the old house come into play again?" asked Jack.

"No, no. It's like he is my only – well, not my only focus – but my first focus. I'm pretty sure once this is done that when I close my eyes I'll see that place again."

Jack's eyes narrowed. "Try to tell me what you see there that draws you," said Jack.

"Look," said Sims. "I don't know. I saw a flash of some photographs. Black and white pictures. They feel important to me, but I don't know why."

Jack looked at Wayne. "Can we talk outside for a minute?"

"What the hell?" asked Sims.

"I've got some personal stuff to talk about if you don't mind," said Jack. "I think I'm sacrificing enough for you."

"Fair enough," said Sims.

Wayne limped around to the back of the car.

"I took some black and whites at the crime scene in Lehigh Acres, Wayne. I'm starting a hobby, so I developed them in my home darkroom."

"So?"

"So, I realize that Sims there couldn't tell time in that morgue drawer, so I can't definitively tie his reanimation to the photographs, but something odd happened with the pictures. The images of Sims and Veselov didn't come out right away. Everything else in the picture did. Everything, clear as a bell."

"Everything but what … their bodies?"

"Yeah. Evidence markers on the floor right beside Sims' body parts came out crisp and clear. The hand right beside it? Black. Nothing."

"Weird. What do you think it means?"

"That's not even the weirdest part. When I got up the next morning, they were perfect. Every part, including the bodies."

"All developed?"

"Yep."

"That's not how it works, Jack."

"I'm aware of that much. You put them in the stop solution and they don't develop any further. These did."

"Anything odd about the camera?"

"Bought it at a thrift store, so as far as I know it's just a camera."

Wayne shook his head. "Feels like we're just makin' shit up now."

"Kathryn Hightower's dead and Veselov is gone. There's a dead cop in the back seat of this car, held together with rebar, baling wire and duct tape, and he's getting impatient. I wish the hell we were making it all up." Jack rubbed his face with his hands. He was exhausted. "I want to ask Sims to elaborate about the pictures, but at the same time I don't want him to become more obsessed with them."

"In case his intuition is right?"

"Rebar in his brain didn't kill him, Wayne. Bullets don't. Dismembering clearly doesn't. Something does, and if it has anything to do with that camera or those photographs, or the negatives, whatever, he can't learn everything because I don't care what you are, self-preservation is always a top priority. He may say he's at our mercy when this all plays out, but in the end, he's powerful enough to kill us both."

Wayne started for the passenger side door again. "Faster we move the faster we get to the end of this night, whatever's gonna happen." He and Jack opened their doors at the same time.

As Jack sat, he said, "The mystery of the reanimated bodies shall remain so for now."

"I'm not comfortable being referred to as a body," said Sims.

Olsen looked at him and raised an eyebrow. "Well, to be more accurate, freakshow, you were a dismembered body. Now you appear to be a smart zombie."

Sims shook his head. "Uncalled for. You need me, Sheriff. I think you know that."

217

"Why do you feel drawn to the photographs?" asked Jack, hoping it wasn't a mistake.

"They're … I think … I don't know." His eyes would not meet Jack's.

"You're fuckin' lying!" shouted Wayne.

"We need to get back to your place and put that question to rest," said Jack. "I'd say we could go to my house, but I have nosy neighbors on both sides of me and across the street."

"At this hour?"

"Any hour. Sims, did it look like the Russian was going anywhere anytime soon?"

"Nah. He was still eating Williams. Had the brain already and –"

"Williams is already dead?" asked Wayne.

"Yes. I thought I made that clear," said Sims.

"You said he was working on him," said Wayne. "I just assumed you meant he was … I don't know, like torturing him or something."

"Believe me, guys. I don't have any vendetta to settle except with Veselov. Besides finding him and killing him, all I can think about is eating. Unfortunately, I am 99.9% certain his flesh is as cold as mine. I don't want to eat him. If he were alive, he'd be my first choice."

"How can you kill him?" asked Jack. "Not only is he huge, he's like you."

"Something tells me I'll know when I am standing physically beside him. Not in any kind of ghostly way like before, when I closed my eyes. I need to be in the room with him to understand how he can die."

"And how you can die, right?"

218

Sims hesitated, then nodded.

"Let me see your arm, Officer Sims," said Jack.

"I appreciate the respect, sir," said Sims, holding out his left arm.

Jack reached up and turned on the overhead light and looked at it, even touching the bumpy, purple flesh that ran clean around his arm. "That's a scab," he said. "Wonder if the bone is stitching as fast."

"If he comes back to full life before we're done tonight, we're really going to have some kind of moral dilemma on our hands," sighed Wayne.

"Shit," said Jack. "I forgot. "You get an address?"

"I did," said Sims. "It's at 1202 SW 25th Street."

"We go there first," said Olsen. "No fuckin' alpaca or rat or poodle stops."

"Pardon me, sir, but you really need to get over that. It helped us. Every one of them."

"Maybe we should make him eat the Russian. Kill two birds with one stone."

"I don't really have a desire for dead flesh."

"You're healing," said Jack. "Maybe he is, too."

"Hurry," said Olsen. "He's a tough enough bastard to catch while he's dead."

*****

It was very late, and Hannah checked the clock again. If Jack were working this late, he would probably not feel like eating when he came home.

It had been a dumb idea. She looked at her things and considered leaving.

You're scared he'll reject you, she thought. *It has nothing to do with the time or breakfast or anything except your fear.*

The realization did nothing to chase away the feeling that she should put everything as it was, take her things and go. She stood there in a long moment of indecisiveness.

Hannah went into the kitchen and to the pantry. She removed the box of cellophane wrap and took it to the counter, tearing off a square for each plate of ingredients she had chopped, prepared and seasoned.

She put them all inside the refrigerator in a stack. She turned off the light in the kitchen, so that it now only glowed a dim blue from the time readout on the microwave oven.

She reached down and grabbed her last bag and her purse, and walked toward Jack Hunger's bedroom.

He might not be hungry when he got home.

At least not for food.

Padding into the room, she left the light off and closed the door behind her. Hannah pulled her blouse over her head and folded it neatly, placing it atop the dresser. She did the same with her pants, and finally, her panties.

She slid underneath the sheets of the detective's bed, forgetting about the negligee she had brought.

Her warm, inviting body would be enough.

In ten minutes, Hannah Maruska was sound asleep.

*****

220

Sergei stared down at the body of Officer Derek Williams. He was ready to turn the torso over. There wasn't much meat on the back because the cop had been in good shape, but the buttocks were fleshy and would take some time to consume.

Sergei felt the strength of a hundred men flowing through him. He had to know if it was his imagination or not. He had torn Williams in half with his bare hands, but by that time much of his meat was gone and the challenge was lessened.

Sergei put down the leg he had been gnawing on and went into the kitchen. He went to the stove and turned on the hood light to see by. It threw a soft, yellow glow over the room.

The refrigerator. He wiped his hands on his pants, the blood soaking into them and smearing up onto his shirt. Sergei then rubbed his hands together to remove the last vestiges of the blood.

Spreading his arms, he stood against the refrigerator and pressed his hands to each side of the large appliance and lifted.

It came off the ground easily. He did it again, but it hit a bank of two cabinets just overhead. Sergei put it back down and stepped back.

With both open palms facing outward, he pushed the refrigerator. It slid back an inch, met resistance, then the wall behind it gave way. Wood splintered and cracked, electrical power surged and shot sparks from the power outlet, lighting up the kitchen like daylight, but Sergei did not stop. He pushed the refrigerator until it smashed into the wall of the hallway behind the kitchen.

Walking forward, he pushed on the wall around the massive hole and it broke away like paper mache, his powerful hands snapping the 2" x 4" beams like toothpicks.

He knew, without question, what it was that fortified him: The flesh. Warm, living, human flesh.

He was not sure the girl would be necessary at all, but Sergei had come to believe the innocent blood of the young had done more to strengthen him than any flesh eaten before or since.

Young Darrin Williams had been a turning point.

He had begun seeing the boy's sister, Sabrina, as a fine bottle of Champagne, only to be opened and consumed for a very special occasion.

He wished he could take a breath. Sergei wanted to know what it smelled like in the house with the girl and all the glorious flesh surrounding him.

He sat on the floor and stared for a moment at the child. She was passed out again. Her father was almost down to bone. After that, Sergei would determine his destination, scoop up the girl and go.

But there would be no rushing the last mouthfuls of the man who had ended his life.

With his consumption, I am recovering my life. His hands ended me; I have regained that life by eating his very body and limbs – perhaps even his soul.

What of the tin man? Someone was helping him; that person or persons had put him back together.

Sims.

He had been there and he had no doubt gotten the address, yet Sergei remained mostly unconcerned.

If I had been able to touch him, I would have torn him apart again, Sergei thought.

He settled in to finish his meal of Williams and wait for the man or men who pursued him. He took another bite from a rib and savored it, even though it was growing cold.

The tin man would be next. And anyone with him.

*****

"There," said Sims. "That place."

"There's the car," said Olsen. "In that field there. See if you can block him in somehow, Jack."

"I can park behind it," he said. "He won't be able to go forward because of that canal."

He pulled onto the vacant lot and drove until the bumper of the vehicle was touching the one driven there by Veselov.

"Okay," gurgled Sims, "let's figure out a plan of attack. I say you two wait out here and let me go in. I'm feeling pretty strong, so if I can surprise him, we may stand a chance."

"You want my gun?" asked Olsen.

Jack snapped his fingers. "Sims, maybe you could shoot out his eyes," said Jack. "He'll be helpless then, even if you can't overpower him. Right? Blind him?"

Sims tried to shrug, but something about the way he had been reassembled ruined the effect. "Not a bad idea. Give me the gun. If everything goes to shit, that's what I'll do."

"Don't shoot the girl by mistake," said Wayne.

"I probably won't have to use it," said Sims. "I'll take it as a precaution. Got a suppressor?"

"Yeah, allow me to pull one from my anus for you," said Wayne.

"You're the sheriff," said Sims. "I have no idea the equipment you can get."

"I prefer to make a big boom when I shoot a perp," said Wayne. "I kinda like people knowing where the trouble is so they can stay away."

"When you get inside, try to crack a blind somewhere so we can monitor the situation," said Jack.

"No need," said Sims. "I saw a skylight. Right over the living room. See if you guys can find a place where you can access the roof. You can lay down and look right in on us."

"Good. Now go," said Olsen. "Jack you give me your gun. As I believe I've said before, I'm a better shot than you."

*****

Sims moved across the vacant lot and Jack and Wayne watched him go to the pool enclosure and try the screen door. The latch clicked lightly and Sims pulled it open.

After stepping in, he closed the door without a sound. He disappeared into the shadows.

They waited for five minutes, only hearing another small click about thirty seconds after he went in.

"I don't have high hopes for this operation," said Wayne.

"Neither do I," agreed Jack. "Trust issues?"

"Nah, I kinda trust him. I just don't think he's big enough or savvy enough to take on Veselov."

"The element of surprise is an advantage-maker."

Something burst out of the dark from their left and landed on top of them before they had a chance to get eyes on it. As Jack struggled to turn his head and get a look, a strong hand pushed his face into the dirt and grass.

Jack heard Wayne struggling for air beside him, and he realized his right arm had slipped free. He reached down to grab his gun, but remembered he'd given it to Wayne.

Jack felt a hand on the right side of his head. He looked left in time to catch a glimpse of Wayne's head rushing toward his, just before a black sheet fell over his eyes.

*****

Sims knelt between the prone bodies of the two unconscious cops, hoping he had not slammed their heads together hard enough to cause brain injury. His action had achieved his goal; they were both knocked out.

He fought the urge to tear away the clothing and feed on them, feeling the sinewy muscle and fat tissue sliding down his throat, providing the strength he would need to fight Veselov. Nothing felt as important as that at the moment.

The skylight had been a good idea. It would be *his* way to take Veselov by surprise. He would not need the strength these good men would provide so long as he had a viable plan instead.

They *were* good men. If not for them, he would be unable to pursue his murderer. He could not achieve his ultimate goal with Detective Jack Hunger awake, though.

Sims had not told the other two officers, but he had gone exploring while sitting quietly in the back seat of the dead girl's Toyota.

During his exploration, he had followed the beckoning call that drew him south within the city of Cape Coral. Sims had again ended up in a small, single-family home, only this time he found a piece of mail.

The name on the letter? Officer Jack Hunger.

It was *his* home. That was where the photographs he continued to see in his mind were stored. He had seen them as clearly as if he were in the room, stacked on the counter, beside the answering machine. The one on top had been of Veselov, and it was taken in the house in Lehigh Acres. Sims knew his photographs were there, too.

They had to be. They were what drew him. He could not tell the men.

Sims subconsciously reached over and touched the scab that had begun to peel away from his right arm. He inspected his left arm with his fingers. He could … feel it now. He check himself for a pulse.

Nothing. Sims tried to take a breath. No. It wasn't possible. Strong, maybe. Alive? Not yet. Maybe when he held the photographs and secured his safety.

Sims fished around Jack's pants and found the keys to the car. He grabbed each man by one arm and dragged them to the car. He used the key to open the trunk.

He wished at that moment that he could smell the girl's body in the trunk, despite her probable decomposition. Even her emaciated remains would give him strength if only he could breathe her in.

With hardly any effort at all, he reached down, lifted Olsen and dropped him atop the emaciated carcass of the young woman. Next, he lay Jack inside. It was not a large trunk, so he had to situate them before being able to close the trunk lid.

Around the pool equipment was a six-foot stucco wall. Sims scaled the wall and crept silently up onto the roof.

*****

Veselov stacked Williams' remains and scooped them up, dropping them into the far corner of the room. Chunks of flesh and gore clung to his clothing, and stained the bandage ready to fall off of his face.

He reached up and peeled it away, feeling the skin beneath with his fingers. Rough, but ... was the hole gone? Yes. It felt that way. He wadded up the bandage and tossed it atop Williams' remains.

Sergei heard a click. He walked back in the living room and looked at the girl. Her breath rose and fell in steady rhythms, and he knelt down beside the girl.

In moments, he found himself stroking the back of her head, fighting the urge to tear her open. He had once loved the idea of having children, but with his brutal life, it was not possible.

He moved away from her to minimize his temptation, and sat cross-legged in the middle of the living room, amidst the pieces of Williams that he had dropped.

Sergei closed his eyes and drifted. He again came upon a single-story ranch home and thought himself inside, taking note of the address number. It was 5020.

Melding into and through the door itself, Sergei felt the rough wood scrape his skin as he stepped through it, even smelling fresh hewn lumber for a brief second.

His senses were tuned beyond what he had ever experienced. Sergei moved deeper into the house and stood in a living area, just opposite a kitchen.

Here. This was his last stop before going to rejoin Krovozhadnost. Sergei saw a closed door ahead of him.

In the next moment, as the thought struck him, he stood inside the room with the closed door, beside a bed. A shape lay beneath the sheets, and the Russian breathed in. In this realm, he could breathe. He could smell. It was glorious.

Coppery sweet. Something else. Perfume? Something else. Bacon. The smell of onion.

An assault on his senses, but not enough to take away his delight at the realization another meal awaited him at his final destination.

Sergei heard what seemed a distant crash. Something landed atop him, knocking him backwards.

The impact was unexpected and Sergei found himself beneath someone, their hands clawing at his face and obscuring his vision. A moment later an explosion boomed in his ears, followed by the sensation of extreme pain and heat shooting through his head. It was followed by a second boom, and more searing heat.

Pain, thought Sergei. *How did I feel that?* It was a more consuming question than who was attacking him and why.

In a sudden realization, Sergei knew he was no longer in his dreamlike state; he was back in the vacant house.

The moment the second explosion had filled his ears, his eyesight became sharply focused, beyond anything he had ever experienced before. Everywhere he looked seemed to be in high definition, crisp and clear.

The tin man whose visage had appeared earlier was there now, and he was on top of him holding a gun. Not for long.

"Get off!" Veselov pistoned his arms outward and felt the weight lift off him. As he heard Sims crash against the wall beside where the girl lay, he stood and brought his hands up to his face. He felt the liquid – no longer cold, but lukewarm – running from the place his eyes once were.

The thought came immediately: *If I have no eyes, how can I see?*

The girl was awake. She stared at Sergei and screamed.

*****

"Where the hell?" asked Jack. His legs were cramped and there was a sickly, copper odor. It smelled of blood and decay.

He was in a trunk. Not much doubt about that.

"Wayne," he said. He felt around and touched his friend's shoulder.

229

Good. He was warm and alive.

"Wayne!" he shouted.

Wayne Olsen's head snapped upward and slammed the inside of the trunk's lid. "Jesus!"

"This had to be Sims," said Jack. "The Russian would've killed us."

"Fuck!" shouted Wayne. "We're fucked! Goddamnit!"

"Relax," said Jack. "Maybe he was worried we'd interfere. We've only treated Sims well so far."

"He knows he's gotta die again when this is all over."

*****

Sims was on his feet a half second after Veselov. By the time he caught his balance, the huge Russian stood right in front of him, his hand on Sims' neck, pushing him against the wall.

No. *Through* the wall. The powerful man with inky black holes where his eyes had once been pushed his head between the wall studs and through the drywall of the adjacent bedroom.

For a moment, his head pushed clean into another room, Sims lost his bearings. The hand around his neck did not hurt, nor did it choke him; he didn't yet breathe.

Yet.

"Stop!" he shouted. "I have … a proposal!"

"A proposal? A fucking proposal? You shoot my fucking eyes out and you have a proposal?"

"Yes! You and I are the same! We're both … unique. We get stronger when we consume the living.

230

We become more and more powerful with each bite, each swallow. Haven't you felt it?"

"I killed you, and you are here to kill me. Simple. There is no proposal." He jerked Sims out of the wall and threw him onto the floor. "Don't get up. I will kill you if you try to stand."

"That's just it!" Shouted Sims. "We're dead, both of us, and you know it! What are you going to do? You killed Derek Williams because he killed you. I know your plan because it was the same as mine. You're going to that house because you're drawn there, just like me. Something there holds the key to everlasting life, eternal power. I believe they are photographs. I've seen them."

Sims was speaking the truth, and what's more, he felt that Veselov knew it. He *was* getting through, and what's more, he was beginning to believe it would be best for him to join with the Russian.

It would be his only way to remain alive. If he continued to heal, he could perhaps ... reappear. His wife wouldn't question it if he looked perfectly alive and well. Victoria would look to God and thank him for his glory. He stared at Veselov. "The house. You've seen it in your mind, haven't you, Mr. Veselov?"

Veselov did not answer.

Sims stared at him for a moment. "Wait a minute. You've already gone there, right? Is that where you were when I surprised you just now?"

"You surprised me in order to kill me."

"I did," said Sims. "Like I said, you killed *your* killer. You know I can't help wanting to kill you, too."

"And you would not be able to stop yourself from trying until you destroyed me." Veselov dropped down

231

and put a knee on top of Sims' chest as he lay on his back on the floor.

"I won't try to kill you," said Sims. "We'll get whatever it is that holds our futures and we can do one of two things. Look."

He reached over and curled his hand around the grip of the .45, surprised that the Russian did not try to stop him.

"Watch. I'm going to shoot myself."

"Allow me," said Veselov, twisting the gun out of Sims' hand. He turned the gun to Sims' midsection and fired.

"Aghh!" shouted Sims. "Shit!"

"You feel it, too," said Veselov. "Pain."

Sims looked down at the hole in his stomach. "What the hell?"

"You bleed mostly black, like me, but now … there is some red."

"I told you, we are the only of our kind," said Sims. "We're healing. We must join together and become unstoppable."

"What use are you to me? I am unstoppable now. Even with your power, you know you cannot defeat me."

Sims thought, then said, "I could defeat any other man. *That's* the point, not whether I could beat you."

"I have only one plan."

"What's that?"

Suddenly, with speed the large man should not possess, he reached down with both hands and snatched Sims' head from his body.

Sims felt himself rising into the air and when he stopped lifting, he stared at Veselov's scarred and ravaged face. He could feel the Russian's hands against the side of his head.

"Mr. Veselov," sputtered Sims, sure he had made the biggest mistake of his ... well, his *afterlife*.

Shooting out the Russian's eyes had only improved his vision. Jack and Wayne had been right, too. His meager strength was nothing in comparison to the well-fed Russian's.

"Do not bother wasting your breath, tin man," said Veselov.

He placed the dead cop's head on the floor beside the girl, who was awake but had her eyes squeezed closed. Sergei could tell. Children were predictable.

*****

Sergei smiled at the severed head of Sims as he plucked the rebar rod out of his neck. As Veselov moved to throw the rod across the room, Sims' hand came up and seized Sergei's wrist.

"Please," the head begged. "Whatever you're going to do ... give me a chance."

"There can be no chances for you. You and your pig friends have been nothing but trouble for me my entire life. If you had your way I would have been executed long ago."

"I'm not who I was. I was just a rookie cop! I hadn't even fired my weapon before."

"You would have. You were on that porch, so brave until I did this." Sergei reached down and tore the right arm from the body. The hand at the end of the sleeved arm contorted and twisted, trying to grab at Veselov.

"This is like holding snake," said the Russian, looking at the arm through his deep, black eye sockets.

Sims' head watched, its expression angry, then confused. "What ... what is that? Is it –"

"Is this ... pure blood?" interrupted Sergei, studying it more closely. "There is some black like before, but now it is even redder than before." He glanced up at the cop's head, but it just looked worried and offered no explanation.

He brought his fingers up to his face. He tasted it and smiled. "I have good news for you and I have bad news for you," said Sergei.

Sims' eyes closed, and blackish-red tears ran down his face.

"Since you do not ask, I will tell you both the good and the bad. The good news is you were healing and perhaps coming back to life. You have some blood within you now, and you no longer feel room temperature."

Sergei waited for a few moments. He raised the arm up to his mouth and bit into it, tearing a six-inch chunk of flesh away from it and chewing it up.

Sims' head winced.

The piece of meat twitched and jerked in Sergei's mouth as though it were alive.

Sergei knew it was. It would live on inside him, as they all would, until absorbed into his flesh.

"The bad news now, I'm afraid.

"Please," muttered Sims. "I can help you."

"The bad news – for you – is that you are now edible."

*****

Jack wasn't sure how much time had passed. They were crammed so tightly into the trunk that they could not shift and they could not reposition more than Jack's one free arm. It was not in the correct position to reach the trunk release lever, even if they knew where it was.

"Can you reach it yet?" asked Wayne.

"Yet? No. Not even close. The girl's body is either on top of it or ... Jesus, I can't even move my left arm, and I can't roll over or anything to get to it."

"We fucked up," said Wayne, a heavy sigh sounding in the dark.

"Time to just start screaming for help?"

"He can't go anywhere," said Wayne. "We're blocking him in."

"Somehow I don't see that as much of an obstacle anymore. If Sims can't put him down or at least out, we won't be able to do anything," said Jack. "If he comes back and we're stuck in here, he'll get to my place one way or another. If he's seeing the same thing Sims is, he'll go to my place if Sims doesn't stop him."

"You really think he'd go after the pictures? You're not even sure if they caused this or not."

Jack stopped talking. His mind jerked in his head like a severed lizard tail. "Shit! Shit! Goddamnit. Wayne, we have to get the hell out of here."

"Why? Well, I know fucking why, but what did you remember?"

235

"Hannah," said Jack. "My cleaning woman."

"Yeah, you said you have the hots for her, so what?"

"I just put the phone call I got from her earlier straight in my head. She's at my place, Wayne."

"You're shittin' me."

"No."

"Is your phone inside the car?" asked Wayne.

"Yeah. Yours?"

"Yeah. I didn't want it ringing and giving us away."

"Same here. You sure we're cops?"

"For now," said Wayne. "Why?"

"We suck. I hope Hannah leaves. Wayne?"

"Yeah?"

"Do you ever pray?"

"Only for rain and shit like that."

"In Florida?"

"I'm giving you an example."

"Okay, then. Pray that Hannah leaves my place, or that she's already gone. I'll be over here doing the same thing."

"Mind if I pray for us, too?"

"Not at all. I hope I wake up in a few minutes."

"Yeah. That's gotta happen, right?" asked Wayne. "This can't be real. None of it."

*****

Sergei found Officer J. Sims to be very satisfying, though he was not sure he felt significantly stronger when he finished consuming his body.

He occasionally glanced at the girl as he ate in silence, wondering if she would add to his strength as the girl's brother had. A black cat had wandered up to the back sliding door, and sat, staring through the glass. Sergei eyed it occasionally. It was bone thin and looked feral.

Every once in a while, he looked over at Sims' head. Sims mostly averted his eyes, but Veselov caught him watching on occasion, terror and defeat in his eyes.

"I have killed you twice, stupid tin man. That gives me an idea."

Sergei stood and picked up a hunk of the meat that had been Officer Justin Sims. On the largest wall, he wrote:

DIE AGAIN TIN MAN

Sergei laughed and it echoed in the vacant home. "You are very quiet. What is the expression?" asked Sergei. "Does a cat have your tongue?"

Sergei bent down and lifted Sims' head from the floor. Sims stared at him wide-eyed, but offered no protest.

"I believe I can make it true," he said, reaching down with his other hand and prying Sims' mouth open.

"No, no!" cried Sims, his words muffled, his mouth filled with the Russian's thick fingers.

Sergei reached inside and pinched the tongue as hard as he could, then ripped it from Sims' mouth. Still holding the dead officer's head, he went to the sliding glass door. The cat did not run. It went to the opening and walked through.

Sergei dropped the plucked tongue on the floor, and the cat quickly snatched it up and ran back outside, disappearing into the night.

Sergei held the head up again and looked into its fading eyes. "I'm afraid you won't be much of a conversationalist. It makes you even more worthless."

Sergei tore the last piece of Officer Justin Sims apart and consumed the last of him.

The girl cried through her duct tape. He picked her up with one powerful arm and carried her out the rear door of the house, leaving it open behind him.

He walked to the field and stared at the cars, instantly recognizing the new vehicle as the Toyota owned by the girl he'd eaten from the petrol station.

Sims did this. Fool to believe that would stop me..

Sergei dropped the girl into the tall grass and knelt beside the small four-door car. He put his left hand against the side and his right palm flat beneath the Toyota and lifted it easily. He hoisted it over his car and tossed it into the canal beyond.

The car floated at first. As it began to take on water, Sergei turned, forgetting about it. He put the girl in the back of the car and started the engine.

His thoughts were now so clear. Sergei now felt as though the individually consumed parts of Sims, his final victim in life, were melding into his very body, the molecules joining as one, making him even stronger than before.

He was off to his final stop. After that, nothing could ever stop him again.

*****

"What the hell?" asked Wayne.

"Feels like we're floating!"

"Yeah, we are," said Wayne. "Water's leaking in under me. Can you find the trunk release?"

Jack tried to move and was surprised to find his arms were both now free, the body of the car's owner and Wayne jammed against the forward wall of the trunk's interior. "I'm searching for it now," he said.

Jack well knew that in the early 2000s, the government mandated that all cars have interior trunk releases, but some were glow-in-the-dark tabs, others were manual switches located behind plastic panels. He wasn't certain what this model had.

Jack's fingers searched and probed. His pants started to get wet and suddenly space in which they were trapped shifted again. Jack found all of his weight on top of Wayne Olsen.

"Shit, Jack!" shouted Wayne. Hurry! I can't fuckin' breathe with you on top of me!"

"I can't … find it!" Jack searched frantically, but to no avail.

"I'm really getting soaked now," said Wayne. "I don't want to drown inside this trunk, Jack. Hurry!"

In the dark, Jack looked for the glowing tab, but either it had been removed or there was a panel of some kind. He reached over his head and found the side panel. There was a latch.

"Found it, I think!" he said, turning the small, plastic release knob. It fell open as he felt the water in the trunk touch his shirt.

"I'm ... having trouble ... keeping my head out of ... the water!" said Wayne.

Jack reached inside the panel and pushed the switch down, and heard a click. Still, the trunk did not open. He reached up and pushed on the lid. It did not move an inch.

"Wayne!" said Jack.

"Yeah?"

"Oh, for Christ's sake, I thought you might be under water."

"In a second ... I will be."

"Take a deep breath, Wayne, and hold it. The water pressure's holding the trunk closed. We're going to have to let the pressure equalize before it'll open."

"Fuck that!" shouted Wayne. "Close your ears!"

Before Jack could figure out what his friend and boss was saying, four gunshots sounded, booming in his ears inside the small space, the hot brass cartridges peppering him. The rounds had done what Wayne intended, however; water started streaming in through the holes. A second later, Jack threw his foot upward and kicked. The pressure equalized somewhat, the trunk sprang open, and water gushed in, filling it in a split-second.

The car quickly sank to the bottom of the 10-foot deep canal, and Jack reached out blindly, grabbing Olsen's arm. He pulled him up and out of the trunk and kicked in his shoes, trying to propel them to the surface.

Jack finally broke through to see the early morning moon shining above them, and Wayne surfaced a split-second later.

They both swam to the seawall on the west bank of the canal. There was a cantilever, concrete dock on the house on the other side of the lot, so Jack helped pull Wayne, with his injured leg, to it.

Jack climbed up the aluminum ladder attached to the dock and pulled Wayne up and out of the water.

Both men collapsed on the concrete and lay on their backs, breathing hard.

"This could not get any more fucked up," said Wayne.

"We're definitely both out of work now," said Jack.

"Maybe in jail."

"Let's go, man. We need a car and we need to get to my house in a hurry."

"He's got a good head start."

"And my phone's in the goddamned car, as is yours," said Jack. "We're going to have to use our authority to get one."

"The people of Cape Coral aren't use to that."

"C'mon," said Jack.

They ran into the street and looked at Veteran's Parkway across the canal. "Let's knock on a door. "C'mon."

Wayne couldn't run, but Jack did. He saw a yellow Mustang in the driveway of a house with overgrown grass and two beat up lawn chairs on the porch. He ran to the door. The porch light was on and Jack saw an overflowing ash tray on a table between them. He picked it up and found a small marijuana roach nestled among the dozens of butts.

Wayne came up behind him. "Probably kids, based on the Mustang out there and this," he said, holding up the roach.

"Knock loud, like a cop."

Jack did. "We look like wet rats."

The door opened and Jack had his wallet out of his pants and showed his badge to the tired looking, 20-something man who answered the door. "What's up, officers? We've been home all night."

"That's not why we're here. We need to use your car, now. Ours was wrecked by a man we were pursuing."

"Dude, I gotta be at work at 8:00 in the morning." He checked his watch. "That's in like five hours."

"This isn't a request," said Wayne. "I'm Sheriff Wayne Olsen, and we need the keys, now."

"Okay, okay," said the young man with a scruffy beard and medium length hair parted in the center. He wore a military green undershirt and camouflage pajama bottoms.

He plodded off and returned a second later, holding them out. "How do I get the car back?"

"Cell phone, too," said Jack. "Hurry. I have to make a call. I won't take it."

Jack realized that in this day and age, people would be more willing to give up their cars than their cell phones.

He brought it to Jack and he dialed Hannah's mobile number.

One ring. Two rings. Three. Her voicemail picked up. Jack stepped off the porch and spoke in a low voice. "Han, it's Jack," he began. "If you're at my place, I need

242

you to get out now. Hurry and get the hell out of there as fast as you can. Someone is on the way there and I'm afraid he'll hurt you if he finds you. Go, now. Please, please I hope you pick up this message."

He disconnected the call and tried his home. It rang a partial time and went straight to the answering machine. He set it to zero rings when he left for work.

"Shit!"

"What is it?" asked Wayne, as he returned to the porch.

Ignoring him, Jack said to the kid, "Do us a favor. Hurry up and write down your work address. Catch a ride to work this morning and I'll personally bring the car back to you. What time do you get off work?"

"Five."

"Okay. I'll have it back to you before you get off. But I'm gonna need to keep your phone."

The kid looked at him. "Shit, are you serious?"

"Sorry."

The kid went to a counter and scribbled the address, giving it to Jack. "Here. Phone and car. You'll really bring them to me tomorrow? Promise?"

"Yeah. Thanks. And please don't tell anyone."

The men left and Wayne went to the passenger side of the Mustang. Jack got in the driver's seat, inserted the key and fired the engine.

"Hang on, Wayne. I'm gonna try to cut this twenty minute drive in half."

*****

243

CHAPTER TEN

Sergei pulled up to the house and drove the car straight into the driveway. It was the exact house he'd seen in his psychic travels, and as he stared at the front door, he felt the powerful draw, beckoning to him.

Inside lies immortality.

He looked at the girl sobbing in the seat beside him. Sergei felt strong. There was no need to waste the powerful energy he knew she would provide. He recalled that when he had "seen" the place, only a woman was there, lying on the bed in a back corner bedroom. Nobody else had been home. Now that Sims was gone, he could afford to save the child for later.

He grabbed Sabrina Williams and took her to the trunk of the car, where he dropped her inside. He would consume her just before his reunion with his former members of Krovozhadnost. Some of them might reject him, he knew. They would not live very long, for he would be surging with strength unlike anything they had ever seen.

He would devour any dissenters in front of the other members. Sergei Veselov would then become a legend among them for the rest of time.

For anybody teetering, he would tell them to shoot him directly in the stomach or chest. If any of them took him up on his challenge, when they were done he would tear one of their arms from its socket and beat them to death with it.

Afterward, he had no doubt they would submit all power to him; he would literally rule them forever.

*****

Hannah awoke with a start. She had heard something. A beep?

She got out of bed and turned on the small fluorescent lamp near the door. She opened the door to the main living area and walked out. She saw the message light flashing on the answering machine.

She pressed 'Play,' but it beeped immediately. No message. She saw a display on the answering machine and pressed the review button. A number appeared, but she did not recognize it.

Hannah went back into her room and found her phone on the nightstand. It was on vibrate. She had also missed a call.

Was it Jack?

She pressed and held the 1 key, and in a moment, was connected to her voicemail. Hannah entered her code and heard Jack's voice.

As she listened, gooseflesh rose on her arms and legs. She did not hesitate. She stuffed the telephone in her purse and collected her clothing from the floor. Jack's voice had sounded frantic, and it had frightened her.

Hannah pulled on her blouse, and reached down to slide her panties up her legs. She stood and pulled them up, followed by her pants and her sandals.

Suddenly, remembering that the number from which Jack had called showed up on her phone, she snatched it from her purse again, opened it and hit dial.

Jack answered in one ring.

"Yeah?"

"Jack?"

"Hannah! It's you! Thank God. Are you at my place?"

"I am, Jack," she said. "I'm sorry, I was going to surprise you and –"

Jack cut her off. "It would have been nice, but I need you to get out of there now. Don't worry about getting any of your things, just go, okay? Do you understand?"

"I do, but Jack –"

"Hannah, go. Just go and get back home. I'll call you later. Promise me!"

"Okay, I'll go."

A sound came at the front door. Someone tried to turn the knob.

"Jack, somebody's here."

"Damnit!" Jack's heart sank. He knew he was at least ten minutes away. She could be dead before they got there.

"Hannah, hurry. In my closet, on the right as you walk in, there's a stepladder –"

246

"I know where it is, Jack," she interrupted. "What then?"

"Open the ladder and put it beneath the attic access hatch in the ceiling. Push the hatch up and get up there, fast."

"What about the ladder? He'll see it!"

"Kick it over or something. Just so it's not obvious if he looks in there. Be sure to close the hatch when you get in the attic."

"He's pushing on the door!"

"Get in the closet and close it. Hurry!"

"I'm going to put the phone in my pocket, Jack, but I'm not hanging up," she whispered.

Hannah turned on the closet light and pulled the stepladder out from behind Jack's crisply ironed shirts. She unfolded it and climbed quickly up the steps, pushing up on the ceiling panel.

It pushed in easily, and Hannah slid it to the side. She glanced around the room.

Coat hangers.

She snatched two of the Carriage Cleaners wire coat hangers and tore the paper off one of them. She caught the tip of the wire and untwisted it, unbending it out to its full length.

She hurried to repeat the process on the other coat hanger and haphazardly twisted them together to make a wire almost 5' long.

Bending one end into a hook, Hannah slipped it under the top rail of the stepladder and twisted it closed.

A loud crack sounded from somewhere in the house. She knew she was running out of time.

Hannah got a bearing on the ladder's location, and while holding onto the coat hanger, she turned off the light, got on the ladder, and hooked the wire around a belt loop on her pants. In five more seconds she was in the attic.

She disconnected the hanger from her shorts and slowly pulled the wire up, feeling the resistant weight of the ladder and hoping it did not straighten the hook and drop to the floor below. Only then did Hannah realize she would have to close the ladder in order for it to fit through the opening.

Sensing the bulky stepladder was almost to the ceiling, Hannah reached down and curled her fingers around the top, aluminum bar. Holding it with her left hand, she found the folding stabilizer supports with her right, popping each of them inward. She felt the ladder collapse.

With a silent sigh of relief, Hanna slowly pulled the stepladder into the attic.

The doorknob below turned. Hannah eyed the hatch lid resting beside the access hole and held her breath as she reached for it.

Light stabbed into the darkness below and a large, shadowy figure filled the doorframe.

*****

The door had been locked, but that would not stop Sergei Veselov. He turned the doorknob with all of his strength, expecting the lock to pop, but it did not. The knob itself stripped and spun freely in his hands.

248

He did not wish to be rushed; it was too important that he have the time to find what he sought without the pressure of the police or other pursuers.

One thing was certain; they would not be searching for Sergei Veselov. He had been reported dead, no doubt. His death was too big a story to be kept out of the press, and if these cops were like any others he had known, they would want to brag about taking him down.

Sergei gave up on the front door after a few moments. If another door was open, he did not need to make it obvious there had been a break-in.

He slipped around to the back sliders. He popped the sliding door lock, but found that other measures had been incorporated by the cop that prevented it from opening. Internal bracing bars and other security mechanisms. He could break it in easily, but again, if the glass shattered, it might alarm the neighbors.

Sergei went back around to the front door, feeling he had wasted precious time. This time, impatience prevailed and he shouldered the door, easily breaking the frame. He then bent the slab outward, curled his fingers between it and the jamb, and pulled the door open with another loud crack.

He stepped into the home's interior and pulled it closed behind him. The door was badly damaged, but from the street it would not be detectable.

Sergei wasn't certain why, but he was surprised to find that he could see perfectly in the pitch dark, even with the black holes for eyes. He moved through the house, past the familiar kitchen and living room and saw the doorway to the bedroom he had seen in his mind's eye.

It was no longer closed as it had been; now the door was open. He walked inside the room. The bed was empty.

Where was the girl who had been sleeping there?

He stopped and stood very still until he heard a slight sound.

He turned from the bedroom and took three steps into the living area again.

Find the photographs. They are your lifeblood.

Sergei did not know what the words meant, only that he would know upon seeing and touching the pictures he was meant to find. He had been drawn there for no other reason.

Another light thud. Sergei looked toward the bedroom he had come from a few seconds before.

He moved toward it and past the bed. The closet door was closed. Sergei turned the knob and pulled it open.

As he pulled the door all the way open and leaned inside, he heard another small thump.

It came from over his head.

Sergei smiled.

*****

Jack floored the accelerator of the 1968 Mustang Fastback, just making the yellow light as the rear end fishtailed around the corner of southbound Santa Barbara Boulevard before straightening out again in the outside lane of eastbound Cape Coral Parkway.

"Keep your shit together, man," wheezed Wayne, his pain worse than before, evident from the expression on his face. "Don't wreck it now."

"I got it," said Jack, grabbing the cell off the seat beside him. He stared at it, then handed it to Wayne. "The connection's still live but she's not saying anything," he said. "I'm afraid to. It's on mute, but if she calls out we'll hear her."

"Almost there, Jack," said Wayne. "We got this, brother."

Jack reached Coronado and cranked the wheel right, the tires sliding only for a moment before catching the pavement and shooting the car south.

Jack saw his street coming up on the right and spun the wheel again. He forced himself to control the vehicle and pulled it onto the front lawn, tossing the seat belt aside as he opened the door in one motion.

He ran to the car and looked inside.

The girl wasn't there.

"C'mon, Wayne!" he called.

He feared the worst with regard to the little girl. Now he could only think of Hannah.

His Hannah.

*****

Hannah sat in the darkness, praying the person who had entered the closet had not seen or heard her as she lowered the panel down over the attic hatch.

She stared at the phone in her hand, seeing that she was still connected to Jack Hunger. That gave her comfort, though she was not certain why. He did not say

251

anything to her, but she thought she could understand why; he didn't want to give away her position.

Her foot became numb beneath her. Nothing could be done.

*****

Sergei moved through the house, shoving things from counters as he searched for what drew him. There was a printer on a table and something told him to look there; he pulled it open, seeing nothing but blank, white paper inside. In anger, he swiped his hand across the counter throwing it across the room where it smashed into the wall.

He no longer cared about noise. Sergei would have what he needed soon, and after that he would ...

He stopped for a moment, considering it. What would he do? Sergei realized it was a question for later.

He moved through the kitchen, following the pull to the other side of the house. He entered an office of some kind and dropped into a desk chair. His hand fell instinctively down to a bag beneath the desk and he lifted the leather portfolio up, placing it on the desk in front of him.

A vibration came over him then; intense and exhilarating, it shook him from his dead marrow to every newly sensitive pore of his skin. In his mind the words echoed, as though spoken through a megaphone into a vast canyon:

You have found everlasting life.

He ripped open the flap and pulled a stack of photographs out.

252

They swam into view as clearly as though he possessed eyes to see them. In all the images, taken from various angles, he was there, on the floor. His legs were splayed out in front of him and a massive wound encompassed his entire chest and abdomen. His left cheek was gone, a mass of shredded tissue clinging to his once strong and handsome face.

Sergei looked down. He raised his shirt and tore away at the many bandages he had wrapped there less than 48 hours before.

He touched the scarred flesh beneath; rough but healed. What was more important was that he felt his own touch.

A thought came over him, and he was compelled to follow through. He searched the desk and found a long, thin letter opener. He plucked it from the cup in which it rested with dozens of pens and pencils and he stabbed it into his stomach.

He sucked air between his teeth – then realized what he had done. He had ... breathed.

Sergei withdrew the letter opener and saw that now it was not only black liquid, but like Sims had demonstrated, it was partially red.

Blood. Human blood. It was warm in his hand, too. He licked the opener with his tongue, cleaning it, and held the narrow, gleaming blade up to his eyes.

He saw his reflection. There, in the center of the dark sockets, were eyes.

Eyes.

Over the outside, tiny eyelids were growing, too. Not quite developed yet, but they were eyelids. He touched the eye again, but this time he jerked backward.

They were sensitive.

He laughed aloud, his big voice no longer gurgling as it had been, but deeper and strong. Sergei looked down to the place he had stabbed himself with the letter opener and saw ... nothing.

No cut. No puncture. Just a remnant of the blood that had run down his stomach and soaked into his pants.

Red blood. I'm not just coming back to life; I'm indestructible.

I am invincible.

He looked again at the photograph of his dead self. His injuries were severe; no wonder the girl had been frightened. Sergei had not realized how he had looked in death. It was something he would never, ever see again.

Nor would anybody else.

Some of the pictures were of Sims' body parts. Sergei stared at them for a few moments, a smile forming on his lips. He had almost achieved perfection when he had torn the tin man with the slight build apart; he was only one limb away.

He dropped the pictures of Sims onto the desk, where the still functioning ceiling fan blew them onto the chair and the floor. He stuffed all the photographs of himself into the portfolio and closed and buckled the strap.

Where was the woman in the bed? Sergei looked toward the front door, but realized that as he asked the very question, an unseen force pulled him toward her.

He followed the sensation, allowing himself to succumb to its knowledge. He found himself back in the bedroom, walking toward the closet. He jerked the door open and stared inside.

Automatically, his eyes moved to an access hatch in the ceiling.

He reached up and pushed it open.

"I know you are up there," he said. "I will give you this chance to come down. If you do not, you will die in the place where you hide."

All at once, Sergei Veselov felt the equivalent of sirens sounding in his brain. A sign of urgency. He needed to get the pictures he held out of this house. Sergei turned and charged into the kitchen, ripping open the drawers until he found what he sought.

A lighter. He ran back to the bedroom and struck the lighter, touching the blue flame to several garments on the clothes hangers. They caught easily. He moved into the living room and lit the sofa. He moved to the corner and saw a case sitting on a table.

All other thoughts left him. He focused on the case. Sergei tucked the portfolio beneath his arm and picked up the solid plastic box with a snap seal. He opened it.

Removing the camera from inside, an intense buzzing overtook his entire body as he held the piece of photographic equipment.

This camera is the source. It is power and life.

Sergei slid it back into the case with reverence and snapped it closed. In the front of the house he heard a screen door slam over the crackling of the spreading fire. He bent down, grabbing the flaming cushions from the sofa and threw them to other parts of the room.

The fire had taken hold now.

He ran toward the sliding glass door and did not stop. His massive body crashed through it and he was outside in the warm, Florida air. He tore through the screen and bolted to the back corner of the house, turned left and ran full speed to the street.

*****

Hannah struggled to breathe. The smoke had seeped into the attic quickly, and while it had been almost suffocating in its warmth before, now she felt her lungs would explode.

She searched through the dense smoke and saw a faint light across the attic. She ducked beneath support wires and stepped over cables and phone lines. As Hannah reached another low beam, her head slammed into one that she had missed that angled sharply down to her right.

Her head swam, dizzy. Blinking her eyes, she struggled to focus and continue her forward momentum toward the faint light.

It would either lead her to a way out and freedom, or it would be the place where she would take her last breath, one consisting of dusty, smoke-filled air.

*****

Olsen's leg was trashed. Infection had likely set in, and putting any weight on it was excruciating.

"Shit!" said Jack. "Wayne, I gotta go find Hannah. Stay in the car if you have to!"

Suddenly, the front window burst outward and smoke and flames licked the exterior stucco wall.

Jack bolted into the screened entry, letting screen slam behind him. The door was splintered in its frame, but it was jammed. Jack tried to grab the doorknob, but it was piping hot. He looked back at Wayne, who was standing outside the car, supporting himself on the door.

"Wayne, try to get to the side of the house. Veselov's here, I know it!"

"You got it, buddy!" shouted Wayne Olsen, and he broke into a sprint, despite the pain Jack knew he was in.

The flames began to pour so heavily through the front windows, Jack knew there would be no way in.

God, let Hannah be alive, he prayed to himself. *Please.*

Running back outside, he reached the side yard in time to watch the enormous frame of Sergei Veselov charging directly into the body of Wayne Olsen, flattening him. Jack reached for his weapon and realized that Wayne still had it.

As the thought entered his mind, Jack watched as Wayne took the gun and rolled onto his stomach to be in a position to fire, emptying the magazine at the retreating Russian mobster. Veselov did not slow, despite the sprays of black-red blood that fanned out behind him with each hit.

The Russian was back in the car.

Where was the little girl? Had he already eaten her?

He ran to his friend and found that Wayne had fallen unconscious. He dropped down to a knee and slapped him in the face, hard.

"Wake up! Wayne, get the fuck up!" He physically pulled his friend up and he awoke as he was being lifted to his feet.

"What the hell happened?"

"Here are the keys! Veselov just took off! Go after him, Wayne. I have to —"

Above their heads, a cracking sound came, and the octagonal grid for his attic vent toppled to the ground. Bare feet appeared in the opening.

"Hannah!" shouted Jack.

Billowing smoke poured out with her feet, eventually obscuring her altogether. She wheezed, "Jack?" Raspy coughing followed, and she did not advance through the opening any farther.

"Wayne go! Go! I'll get Hannah!"

Wayne grabbed the keys from Jack's hands and limped toward the car. He got inside and fired the engine. It was in reverse and the tires squealed down the street before Jack reached the shed in the back of the house.

He didn't have a key with him, so Jack just kicked the door with all his might, finally snapping the hinges. He muscled the door aside and reached in, grabbing his extension ladder.

Out of breath but not caring, he charged toward the vent and leaned the ladder against the side of the house. He locked it in and scrambled up the rungs. When he reached Hannah's legs, he tucked them beneath his arms and pulled her out, carefully easing her across the top of the ladder and feeding her legs down until her head emerged and her feet were firmly planted on the ladder steps.

He was dizzy from the effort, but managed, "My God, Hannah, I'm so happy you're alive."

She was covered with sweat and her face was dusted with soot and insulation. "Jack, it was horrible. I heard his voice, and he sounded Russian. I think whoever it is must be retaliating for the man who was killed in Lehigh Acres."

"Han, it wasn't just a member of Krovozhadnost. It was Veselov," said Jack, stepping down the ladder and holding onto her legs as she came down behind him. They reached the bottom and she stepped onto the grass.

Jack pulled her into his arms and held her. A moment later – it could've been five minutes – she said, "I thought you said Veselov was dead."

Jack held her again. "I'm hoping that will be true again," he whispered.

*****

Wayne Olsen drove, alternately wiping the sweat from his forehead and blinking his eyes to focus. He never lost the taillights of the Malibu, which was now about a quarter mile ahead of him.

He brought his foot farther down and the 289 responded, the headers pop-pop-popping down Del Prado like the powerful hotrod it was. Wayne saw Veselov crank it right onto the Midpoint Bridge, and within fifteen seconds, he was there himself.

The toll gates had been removed from the bridge exiting town, so Wayne could not hope for that delay to help him chase down the Russian. He made the turn and floored it now, bringing the Mustang up to seventy-five miles an hour fast.

The Malibu was now less than an eighth of a mile away. He reached eighty, and he closed the gap just before the center of the mile-long bridge.

Two lanes traversed the Caloosahatchee, and now Wayne pulled alongside the big Russian. He held his empty gun in his right hand and pointed it at Veselov, who glanced over and laughed at the sight. The mobster yelled something, but Wayne did not hear anything over the roar of the Mustang's engine. There were no automatic windows in the vehicle, and he couldn't reach the crank handle to lower it.

Veselov cranked the wheel hard and smashed into the side of the Mustang. Wayne, taken by surprise, crashed into the left guard rail, bounced off and regained control of the car. He had fallen back, so he floored the accelerator again and caught up.

Veselov slammed on the brakes this time. When he slowed, he cranked the car hard left, then hard right again, smashing into the right hand guard rail, but not breaking through it.

What the hell is he trying to do? Go over the edge? Is the girl in the car? Shit!

Wayne wasn't sure what to do. He looked ahead and saw there was about an eighth of a mile left over the water. He floored it and drew up next to Veselov once more.

*****

Inside the home of Jack Hunger, the flames licked at the desk, engulfing everything on top of it. As the flames crawled across the floor, they touched the corner of the stack of photographs of Officer Justin Sims, the last meal of Sergei Veselov.

The photograph on top, which was of Sims' severed head, burned and curled away to reveal the officer's left leg. Bubbling and popping, the image curled in on itself, and beneath that was the torso and the one remaining limb that had still been attached to the rookie cop.

One by one, the immortality of Justin Sims seared away.

*****

As Wayne struggled to keep the vehicle even with the Malibu, he glanced inside the car. Veselov had stopped trying to run him off the road now. In fact, he gripped the steering wheel with both hands and was slowing down.

Something was wrong with him. Wayne squinted, now turning his Mustang into the side of the Malibu, pressing his car into the other, pushing him flat against the right guard wall, the steel automobile sparking and grinding against the concrete barrier.

Wayne saw police lights behind him. Word had gotten out. He cranked the wheel hard again, and as he saw the Malibu come to a full stop, Veselov smashed out the side window and crawled out.

He stood staring at Wayne, who did not get out of his car. The Russian had a yellowish glow to him, and he stared at the sky and screamed at the top of his lungs. His chest and stomach burst into flames. Wayne's mouth hung open.

Next, as Veselov moved around to the rear of the car and hooked his fingers beneath the trunk lid, he tore it open, twisting the metal with his bare hands and flinging it off the side of the bridge.

His arms and hands were not yet burning, but the rest of his body was engulfed. He held a plastic case of some kind and what appeared to be a portfolio. Still holding onto those items, he reached down inside the trunk and yanked the writhing body of the girl out.

"Stop, Veselov!" Wayne shouted, but as he watched, the inferno that was Sergei Veselov took three steps, threw one flaming foot on the north barrier and leapt from the bridge, plummeting into the water forty feet below.

Wayne did not stop to think. He limped to the side, took one glance at the police car that had just slid to a stop twenty yards away, and followed the Russian and his little captive, leaping over the barrier, dropping through the air feet first.

The drop seemed to take forever, and when he hit, he plunged into the tepid waters of the Caloosahatchee.

*****

Veselov managed to keep his grip on the girl as he fell, but when he impacted the river's water, everything was ripped free from his arms.

The water extinguished the exterior flames, but the heat burning inside him was scorching hot. He felt his very brain was on fire, and he could smell his charred flesh. He could not think clearly! It felt as though his very soul was sunken in molten lava.

An enormous splash broke the water ten feet away. He did not see the source, but guessed it was the man who had been chasing him. He did not care. He could kill him in seconds. He needed ... Sergei looked all around him.

The man surfaced five feet away, searched frantically, then dove down into the water. When Sergei had jumped in, he realized the river was not very deep.

Less than five seconds later, the man surfaced with the child in his arms. He saw Veselov looking at him, and a bright spotlight clicked on, illuminating all of them, as well as the surrounding waters.

The man with the police officer's daughter in his arms screamed up at the officer holding the spotlight, "Radio for a boat to get over here now! I have a child who needs help! Hurry!"

The cop above them hesitated for a brief moment before disappearing beyond the guardrail. Veselov searched for the most important item he had lost.

As the man holding the girl treaded water fifteen feet away from him, Veselov threw his right arm forward and began to close the gap between them.

If he could consume the girl quickly, it might save him.

*****

When the Russian was less than ten feet away, Wayne realized he was exhausted. Holding the girl would be hard enough, but treading water at the same time was a test of his endurance.

Something bumped his arm. Wayne screamed, pushing back, shifting the girl to his other arm, and saw it was not the bull shark he feared, but something flat and dark, almost blending into the water.

Was it what Veselov had been carrying when he jumped into the river? Wayne snatched it from the water and kicked several more times in an attempt to open up more distance between him and the Russian. It would be impossible. The girl had to help him.

"I'm going to move you around and tear the tape off your hands," whispered Wayne. "Understand? You're going to be safe, okay?"

The girl shook her head no, but she answered him; that meant she was better than Wayne expected. He managed to tear the duct tape from her wrists. He then peeled the strip from her mouth.

"Okay, honey. I know your arms are probably tired, but I need you to hook them around my neck from behind and hold on tight," he said.

Veselov was five feet away now, his eyes on the leather pouch Wayne held. He kicked four or five more times. The Russian glowed yellow-red and water hissed and popped around him. His face was now almost black, like charcoal.

Wayne ripped open the package and pulled out a stack of water-soaked photographs. They were of Sergei Veselov after the shooting. Black and white shots. Dead. Very dead.

"No!" shouted Veselov. "Give them to me!"

"Hell no!" shouted Wayne, and he put the corner of one in his mouth and tore it in two.

Less than five feet away, the Russian's arm, as though with a life of its own, ripped free from his body. He stared in horror.

Wayne did, too. He watched, and kicked to stay afloat. The police boat's engine sounded in the distance. Sergei Veselov was making no more forward progress, but the flow of the river kept the two men generally the same distance apart.

Wayne flipped through the images and found another. He pulled it out and this time he focused on the location of the tear. He ripped the picture down the center, and as he watched, Veselov's head split down the middle, his blackish-red, inky bodily fluids ran like a waterfall into the river in which he now floated. He screamed as his head split from the top, but by the time his mouth and chin tore in two, he had lost the power to cry out.

Wayne dipped all of the pictures in the water again, soaking them thoroughly, then he systematically tore them into pieces, watching the once massive Russian dismembering before him as though by magic.

Wayne gathered as many of the remainders as he could, wadded them up and stuffed them back into the leather bag. The police boat drove up behind him and he paddled there, exhausted but relieved.

They pulled the girl aboard first.

Wayne floated there for a moment, unable to keep himself afloat. As he felt himself sinking, a hand clutched his collar and pulled him back up.

He managed to hook a hand over the edge of the police boat and he clung there and cried.

"You okay Sheriff?" asked the Cape Coral cop. "What happened? Where did the guy go?"

"I don't know," panted Wayne. "I don't know where he is."

He knew it would take a good long time to make up anything that would sound convincing.

In the end, he said nothing except, "This is Derek Williams' daughter."

They would just have to figure out the rest.

*****

EPILOGUE

The boy poked a long stick at the charred carcass lying beside the mangroves on the edge of the canal on 25th Street.

"Get away from that, son," his father said.

"Dad, this cat looks like it was on fire," said Billy.

"I'll call the City and report it," said his dad. "Damned sick kids."

*****

Jack Hunger left the police force the day following the conclusion of the investigation. In the end, he and Wayne Olsen acted as mystified as everyone else as to what had happened to Justin Sims and Sergei Veselov.

Nobody bought it. There wasn't enough proof and in the end, the evidence pointed to the impossible. In the end, both men resigned with full pensions.

The camera had disappeared and Jack hoped it was destroyed or resting at the bottom of the river. Veselov's body was also never recovered, and it was assumed to have continued to burn from the inside until it was pure ash; floating silt at the bottom of the Gulf waters.

Wayne told Jack that he had realized the reason Veselov was burning the moment he tore the photograph. They had not known what had happened to Sims until Wayne had put two and two together.

Veselov had *eaten* Sims. The images of Sims had burned, and so had every vestige of the man himself.

He was burning inside the Russian. The Krovozhadnost kingpin had been powerless to stop his own internal combustion as every piece of Sims burst into flame. Even had he not leapt into the river, and even if Wayne had never found the portfolio and begun to dismember him by proxy of the photographs, he would eventually have become a lump of char.

Jack and Hannah finally had their date and it became much more than that. Ex-cop Hunger also did what he could to research the history of the missing Pentax. He had the original manual at home, and found the serial number among the documentation.

With Wayne's help, he researched it. It did not take him very long to track down the original purchaser of the photographic equipment.

It was a man named Stan Richardson. He'd bought the camera right there in Cape Coral.

When Jack and Wayne discovered how Richardson had died, and how his body had been discovered with that of Gil Bellows, an infamous serial rapist and murderer, they shared chills down their spines.

The trail went dead from there. No way to trace the camera's history any further, at least for the moment.

*****

Two months later, a man walked along the beach on Sanibel Island, and saw something sticking up from the sand. He carried his burlap sack and a small aluminum shovel over and pried it free. It was a plastic case of some kind, and it appeared to be in excellent shape.

"Honey, come here! I think I found some treasure!"

Marion ran over. "What is it?"

"Not sure yet," said Don Shulman, holding it up. "It's pretty heavy. Wonder what's in it."

"Hurry up," said his wife. "Open it."

He flipped the latches and tried to pull it open. The gap where it sealed was crusted over with sand and corrosion from its time in the Gulf waters. He pulled out a small pocket knife and pried until the seal broke.

"It's a camera!" he said, sliding it out. "Judging from the case, it's been floating around out there a while. It's dry as a bone inside and the camera's really clean. He pulled something out and opened the small, drawstring bag.

"Lenses, too!"

"Any name in there? Maybe of the owner?" Marion asked.

He looked. "Nothing. Finder's keepers, I guess."

"Great way to end our vacation!" she said.

That evening, they purchased film for their new camera. It would be perhaps the coolest story they would tell upon their return to Fort Worth, Texas. They had found shells, too. Many beautiful seashells.

"Hey, M," said Don. "Maybe when we come back in June for Ed and Allyson's wedding I can use this to get some cool spontaneous shots. You know, put together a cool Shutterfly album or something."

Marion's face lit up. "We could give them as gifts to the family. Perfect."

"You'll have to practice when you get home so you know what you're doing."

Don and Marion left the beach, hauling their treasure tucked inside their beach bags.

They had no way of knowing that they would never again return to Naples, Florida.

THE END

Keep an eye out for the sequel to The Camera: Bloodthirst, coming in 2015!

Flash Fiction Contest Winners

If you follow me on Facebook, you know I often run contests and giveaways. One of my most brilliant ideas was during my reign at Zombie Book of the Month Club's page. I was very honored to have won the award for the month of August, 2014 for the Dead Hunger zombie series, which, at the time, stood at seven books. The emblem is to the right, just in case you don't believe me! Anyway, I held a flash fiction contest during that month, and had quite a few  excellent entries. The rules? Write a horror story in 100 words or less. The winner of the contest was to receive a one-time publishing contract with my company, Dolphin Moon Publishing, and their story would appear at the end of my next book – and this is it! So after the words "The End," you will have the pleasure of reading the winning story, "A Mother's Love," by Amanda Barnett, the 2nd place story, "I Don't Camp," by Rebecca Parker, and the 3rd place story, "Fertilizer," by Justin Dunne and Jeff Clare. Congratulations to the winners and thanks to everyone for all of your wonderful support.

GRAND PRIZE WINNER

A Mother's Love
By Amanda Barnett

A mother's love is a protective gift.

My mantra ran through my head each night. It had worked for weeks, but now the shadows in my mind were screaming for their release. I could feel them slipping in, showing me all the ways they were going to hurt my family.

I continued down the hall, pausing by my son's room, stroking an errant curl from his forehead, and hoping even in slumber that he could feel my love.

I hurried down the hallway, climbed onto the windowsill, and took the dark step to save my family from my shadows.

Amanda Barnett is a 34-year-old mother from southeastern Kentucky. She has always loved a good monster story, especially of the brain-devouring variety!

SECOND PLACE

I Don't Camp
By Rebecca Parker

"Come camping with us," they said.

"It will be fun," they insisted.

"You never come with us," they whined.

So, I went this time and it has been fun. We had a campfire, a few beers and some very burnt hotdogs.

It was all going so well until my friends started to disappear.

At first I didn't really notice. Hey, there were ten of us here and I am *not* the babysitter.

I'm pretty sure I'm next – since I *am* the only one left here now.

Well, maybe, maybe not … I do black out sometimes …

Rebecca Parker is a 47-year-old wife and mother from the Pacific Northwest. She began reading Stephen King's books at age twelve, and has not been right since …

273

THIRD PLACE

Russian Roulette
By Jeff Clare & Justin Dunne

Spinnnn ...

"This world may survive, but we ain't made for a future."

Eyes closed ... CLICK. "Shit...fuck!"

"We can fertilize it though. Put another bullet in?"

Shrugging, "Would if I could, lil' brother. Only one of us getting the easy way out."

Dead hands scratch at the bathroom door. *Spinnnn* ...

"Man, that doesn't even scare me anymore, just pisses me off. Give us a fucking minute!" Breath held ...CLICK. "AH...shit."

Door rattles on its hinges.

"Want me to point this one at you?"

Spinnnnn ...

Nodding, "Manifest destiny, big bro."

"When you see mom, up there, you tell her...I'm sorry."

Spinnnn ...

Click, click, BOOM!

(Author Photographs and biographies are located on the following page.)

Jeff Clare, from the northern valleys of Kentucky, is a publisher, a children's therapist, musician, and the founder/owner of the Facebook group All Things Zombie.

Justin Dunne likes his zombies and likes to play with words. In his den on the West Coast of Australia, he often likes to combine the two!

THE COMPLETE WORKS OF AUTHOR ERIC A. SHELMAN

(Updated October 4, 2014)

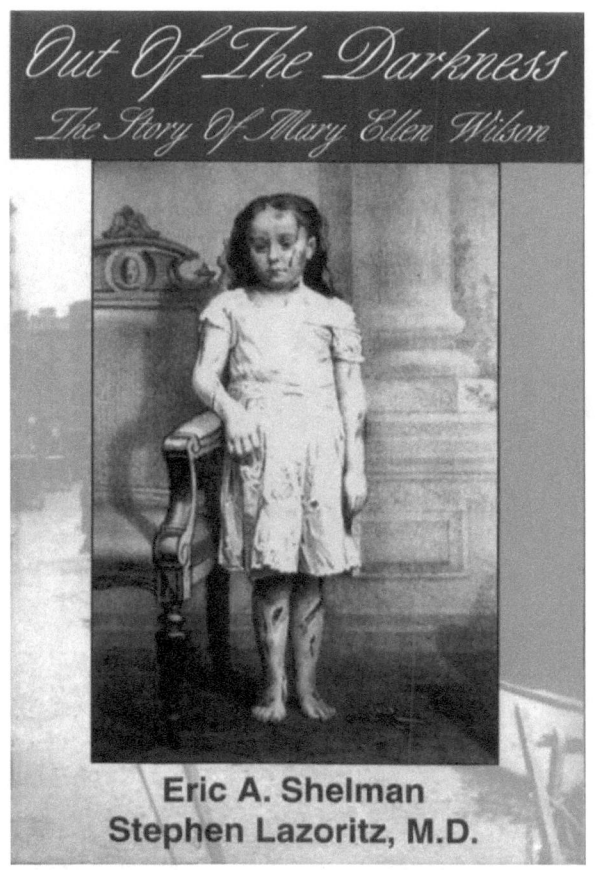

www.ingramcontent.com/pod-product-compliance
Lightning Source LLC
Chambersburg PA
CBHW020347180626
46812CB00001B/369